The Truth About Tristrem Varick

A Novel

Edgar Saltus

Alpha Editions

This edition published in 2024

ISBN : 9789362517531

Design and Setting By
Alpha Editions
www.alphaedis.com
Email - info@alphaedis.com

As per information held with us this book is in Public Domain.
This book is a reproduction of an important historical work. Alpha Editions uses the best technology to reproduce historical work in the same manner it was first published to preserve its original nature. Any marks or number seen are left intentionally to preserve its true form.

Contents

I.	- 1 -
II.	- 5 -
III.	- 12 -
IV.	- 19 -
V.	- 25 -
VI.	- 31 -
VII.	- 36 -
VIII.	- 44 -
IX.	- 50 -
X.	- 53 -
XI.	- 59 -
XII.	- 65 -
XIII.	- 71 -
XIV.	- 76 -
XV.	- 82 -
XVI.	- 87 -
XVII.	- 93 -

I.

It is just as well to say at the onset that the tragedy in which Tristrem Varick was the central figure has not been rightly understood. The world in which he lived, as well as the newspaper public, have had but one theory between them to account for it, and that theory is that Tristrem Varick was insane. Tristrem Varick was not insane. He had, perhaps, a fibre more or a fibre less than the ordinary run of men; that something, in fact, which is the prime factor of individuality and differentiates the possessor from the herd; but to call him insane is nonsense. If he were, it is a pity that there are not more lunatics like him.

It may be that the course of conduct which he pursued in regard to his father's estate served as basis to the theory alluded to. At the time being, it created quite a little stir; it was looked upon as a piece of old-world folly, an eccentricity worthy of the red-heeled days of seigneurial France, and, as such, altogether out of place in a money-getting age like our own. But it was not until after the tragedy that his behavior in that particular was brought up in evidence against him.

The facts in the case were these: Tristrem's father, Erastus Varick, was a man of large wealth, who, when well on in the forties, married a girl young enough to be his daughter. The lady in question was the only child of a neighbor, Mr. Dirck Van Norden by name, and very pretty is she said to have been. Before the wedding Erastus Varick had his house, which was situated in Waverley Place, refurbished from cellar to garret; he had the parlor—there were parlors in those days—fitted up in white and gold, in the style known as that of the First Empire. The old Dutch furniture, black with age and hair-cloth, was banished. The walls were plastered with a lime cement of peculiar brilliance. The floors of the bedrooms were carpeted with rugs that extended under the beds, a novelty in New York, and the bedsteads themselves, which were vast enough to make coffins for ten people, were curtained with chintz patterns manufactured in Manchester to frighten children. In brief, Erastus Varick succeeded in making the house even less attractive than before, and altogether acted like a man in love.

After three years of marriage, Tristrem was born and Mrs. Varick died. The boy had the best of care and everything that money could procure. He was given that liberal education which usually unfits the recipient for making so much as his bread and butter, and at school, at college, and when he went abroad his supply of funds was of the amplest description. Shortly after his return from foreign lands Erastus Varick was gathered to his fathers. By his will he bequeathed to Tristrem a Panama hat and a bundle of letters. The rest and residue of his property he devised to the St. Nicholas Hospital. The value of that property amounted to seven million dollars.

Now Dirck Van Norden had not yet moved from the neighborhood to a better place. Tristrem was his only grandson, and when he learned of the tenor of the will, he shook his fist at himself in the looking-glass and swore, in a bountiful old-fashioned manner which was peculiar to him, that his grandson should not be divested of his rights. He set the lawyers to work, and the lawyers were not long in discovering a flaw which, through a wise provision of the legislature, rendered the will null and void. The Hospital made a bold fight. It was shown beyond peradventure that from the time of Tristrem's birth the intention of the testator—and the intention of a testator is what the court most considers—had been to leave his property to a charitable institution. It was proved that he had made other wills of a similar character, and that he had successively destroyed them as his mind changed in regard to minor details and distributions of the trust. But the wise law was there, and there too were the wise lawyers. The decision was made in accordance with the statute, and the estate reverted to Tristrem, who then succeeded in surprising New York. Of his own free will he made over the entire property to the account of the Hospital to which it had been originally devised, and it was in connection with that transfer that he was taxed with old-world folly. But the matter was misunderstood and afterward forgotten, and only raked up again when the press of two continents busied itself with his name. At that time he was in his twenty-fifth or twenty-sixth year.

He was slender, of medium height, blue of eye, and clear-featured. His hair, which was light in color, he wore brushed upward and back from the forehead. When he walked, it was with a slight stoop, which was the more noticeable in that, being nearsighted, he had a way of holding his chin out and raising his eyebrows as though he were peering at something which he could not quite discern. In his face there was a charm that grew and delighted and fastened on the beholder. At the age of twenty-six he would have been recognized by anyone who had known him as a boy. He had expanded, of course, and a stoop and dimness of vision had come with years; but in his face was the same unmistakable, almost childish, expression of sweet good-will.

His school-days were passed at Concord. When he first appeared there he looked so much like a pretty girl, in his manner was such gentleness, and his nature was found to be so vibrant and sensitive, that his baptismal name was promptly shortened into Trissy. But by the time he reached the fourth form it was lengthened back again to its rightful shape. This change was the result of an evolution of opinion. One day while some companions, with whom he happened to be loitering, scurried behind a fence, he stopped a runaway horse, clinging to the bridle though his arm had been dislocated in the earliest effort. Another time, when a comrade had been visited, unjustly it appeared, with some terrible punishment—five hundred lines, perhaps, or something equally direful—Tristrem made straight for the master, and argued with him to such effect that the punishment was remitted. And again, when a tutor asked how it was that there was no W in the French language, Tristrem answered, "Because of Waterloo."

Boys are generous in their enthusiasms; they like bravery, they are not deaf to wit, but perhaps of all other things they admire justice most. And Tristrem seemed to exhale it. It is said that everyone has a particular talent for some one thing, whether for good or evil, and the particular talent which was accorded to Tristrem Varick was that of appreciation. He was a born umpire. In disputes his school-fellows turned to him naturally, and accepted his verdict without question. When he reached the altitudes which the Upper School offers, no other boy at St. Paul's was better liked than he. At that time the form of which he was a member—and in which, parenthetically, he ranked rather low—was strengthened by a new-comer, a turbulent, precocious boy who had been expelled from two other schools, and with whom, so ran the gossip, it would go hard were he expelled again. His name was Royal Weldon, and on his watch, and on a seal ring which he wore on his little finger, he displayed an elaborate coat-of-arms under which for legend were the words, *Well done, Weldon,* words which it was reported an English king had bawled in battle, ennobling as he did so the earliest Weldon known to fame.

Between the two lads, and despite the dissimilarity of their natures, or perhaps precisely on that account, there sprang up a warm friendship which propinquity cemented, for chance or the master had given them a room in common. At first, Tristrem fairly blinked at Weldon's precocity, and Weldon, who was accustomed to be admired, took to Tristrem not unkindly on that account. But after a time Tristrem ceased to blink and began to lecture, not priggishly at all, but in a persuasive manner that was hard to resist. For Weldon was prone to get into difficulties, and equally prone to make the difficulties worse than they need have been. When cross-questioned he would decline to answer; it was a trick he had. Now Tristrem never got into difficulties, except with Latin prosody or a Greek root, and he was frank to a fault.

It so happened that one day the headmaster summoned Tristrem to him. "My dear," he said, "Royal is not acting quite as he should, is he?" To this Tristrem made no reply. "He is a motherless boy," the master continued, "a poor motherless boy. I wish, Tristrem, that you would use your influence with him. I see but one course open to me, unless he does better—" Tristrem was a motherless boy himself, but he answered bravely that he would do what he could. That evening, as he was battling with the platitudes of that

Augustan bore who is called the Bard of Mantua, presumably because he was born in Andes—Weldon came in, smelling of tobacco and drink. It was evident that he had been to town.

Tristrem looked up from his task, and as he looked he heard the step of a tutor in the hall. He knew, if the tutor had speech with Weldon, that on the morrow Weldon would leave the school. In a second he had seated him before the open dictionary, and in another second he was kneeling at his own bedside. Hardly had he bowed his head when there came a rap at the door, the tutor entered, saw the kneeling figure, apologized in a whisper, and withdrew.

When Tristrem stood up again, Weldon was sobered and very pale. "Tristrem—" he began, but Tristrem interrupted him. "There, don't say anything, and don't do it again. To-morrow you had better talk it over with the doctor."

Weldon declined to talk it over with anyone, but after that he behaved himself with something approaching propriety. Two years later, in company with his friend, he entered Harvard, from which institution he was subsequently dropped.

Tristrem meanwhile struggled through the allotted four years. He was not brilliant in his studies, the memorizing of abstruse questions and recondite problems was not to his liking. He preferred modern tongues to dead languages, an intricate fugue was more to his taste than the simplest equation, and to his shame it must be noted that he read Petrarch at night. But, though the curriculum was not entirely to his fancy, he was conscientious and did his best. There are answers that he gave in class that are quoted still, tangential flights that startled the listeners into new conceptions of threadbare themes, totally different from the usual cut and dried response that is learned by rote. And at times he would display an ignorance, a stupidity even, that was fathomless in its abysses.

After graduation, he went abroad. England seemed to him like a rose in bloom, but when autumn came and with it a succession of fogs, each more depressing than the last, he fled to Italy, and wandered among her ghosts and treasuries, and then drifted up again through Germany, to Paris, where he gave his mornings to the Sorbonne and his evenings to orchestra-stalls.

II.

It was after an absence of nearly five years that Tristrem Varick returned to the States. He had wearied of foreign lands, and for some time previous he had thought of New York in such wise that it had grown in his mind, and in the growing it had assumed a variety of attractive attributes. He was, therefore, much pleased at the prospect of renewing his acquaintance with Fifth Avenue, and during the homeward journey he pictured to himself the advantages which his native city possessed over any other which he had visited.

He had not, however, been many hours on shore before he found that Fifth Avenue had shrunk. In some unaccountable way the streets had lost their charm, the city seemed provincial. He was perplexed at the discovery that the uniform if depthless civility of older civilizations was rarely observable; he was chagrined to find that the *minutiæ* which, abroad, he had accepted as a matter of course, the thousand trifles which amount, after all, to nothing particularly indispensable, but which serve to make mere existence pleasant, were, when not overlooked, inhibited by statute or custom.

In the course of a week he was surprised into reflecting that, while no other country was more naturally and bountifully favored than his own, there was yet no other where the art of living was as vexatiously misunderstood.

Of these impressions he said nothing. His father asked him no questions, nor did he manifest a desire for any larger sociological information than that which he already possessed. His grandfather was too irascible for anyone to venture with in safety through the shallows of European refinements, and of other relatives Tristrem could not boast. Few of his former friends were at once discoverable, and of those that he encountered some had fallen into the rut and routine of business life, some had married and sent in their resignations to everything but the Humdrum, and some passed their days in an effort to catch a train.

For the moment, therefore, there was no one to whom Tristrem could confide his earliest impressions, and in a month's time the force of these impressions waned; the difference between New York and Paris lost much of its accent, and in its place came a growing admiration for the pluck and power of the nation, an expanding enthusiasm for the stretch and splendor of the land.

During the month that followed, an incident occurred which riveted his patriotism forever. First among the friends and acquaintances whom Tristrem sought on his return was Royal Weldon. Outwardly the handsome, turbulent boy had developed into an admirable specimen of manhood, he had become one on whom the feminine eye likes to linger, and in whose companionship men feel themselves refreshed. His face was beardless and unmustached, and into it had come that strength which the old prints give to Karl Martel. In the ample jaw and straight lips was a message which a physiognomist would interpret as a promise of successful enterprise, whether of good or evil. It was a face which a Crusader might have possessed, or a pirate of the Spanish main. In a word, he looked like a man who might be a hero to his valet.

Yet, despite this adventurous type of countenance, Weldon's mode of life was seemingly conventional. Shortly after the removal from Harvard, his father was mangled in a railway accident and left the planet and little behind him save debts and dislike. Promptly thereupon Royal Weldon set out to conquer the Stock Exchange. For three years he grit his teeth, and earned fifteen dollars a week. At the end of that period he had succeeded in two things. He had captured the confidence of a prominent financier, and the affection of the financier's daughter. In another twelvemonth he was partner of the one, husband of the other, and the taxpayer of a house in Gramercy Park.

Of these vicissitudes Tristrem had been necessarily informed. During the penury of his friend he had aided him to a not inconsiderable extent; though afar, he had followed his career with affectionate interest, and the day before Weldon's wedding he had caused Tiffany to send the bride a service of silver which was mentioned by the reporters as "elegant" and "chaste." On returning to New York, Tristrem naturally found the door of the house in Gramercy Park wide open, and it came about that it was in that house that his wavering patriotism was riveted.

This event, after the fashion of extraordinary occurrences, happened in a commonplace manner. One Sunday evening he was bidden there to dine. He had broken bread in the house many times before, but the bread breaking had been informal. On this particular occasion, however, other guests had been invited, and Tristrem was given to understand that he would meet some agreeable people.

When he entered the drawing-room, he discovered that of the guests of the evening he was the first to arrive. Even Weldon was not visible; but Mrs. Weldon was, and, as Tristrem entered, she rose from a straight-backed chair in which she had been seated, and greeted him with a smile which she had copied from a chromo.

Mrs. Weldon was exceedingly pretty. She was probably twenty-two or twenty-three years of age, and her intellect was that of a girl of twelve. Her manner was arch and noticeably affected. She had an enervating way of asking unnecessary questions, and of laughing as though it hurt her. On the subject of dress she was very voluble; in brief, she was prettiness and insipidity personified—the sort of woman that ought to be gagged and kept in bed with a doll.

She gave Tristrem a little hand gloved with *Suède*, and asked him had he been at church that morning. Tristrem found a seat, and replied that he had not. "But don't you like to go?" she inquired, emphasizing each word of the question, and ending up with her irritating laugh.

"He does," came a voice from the door and Weldon entered. "He does, but he can resist the temptation." Then there was more conversation of the before-dinner kind, and during its progress the door opened again, and a young girl crossed the room.

She was dressed in a gown of canary, draped with madeira and fluttered with lace. Her arms and neck were bare, and unjewelled. Her hair was Cimmerian, the black of basalt that knows no shade more dark, and it was arranged in such wise that it fell on either side of the forehead, circling a little space above the ear, and then wound into a coil on the neck. This arrangement was not modish, but it was becoming—the only arrangement, in fact, that would have befitted her features, which resembled those of the Cleopatra unearthed by Lieutenant Gorringe. Her eyes were not oval, but round, and they were amber as those of leopards, the yellow of living gold. The corners of her mouth drooped a little, and the mouth itself was rather large than small. When she laughed one could see her tongue; it was like an inner cut of watermelon, and sometimes, when she was silent, the point of it caressed her under lip. Her skin was of that quality which artificial light makes radiant, and yet of which the real delicacy is only apparent by day. She just lacked being tall, and in her face and about her bare arms and neck was the perfume of health. She moved indolently, with a grace of her own. She was not yet twenty, a festival of beauty in the festival of life.

At the rustle of her dress Tristrem had arisen. As the girl crossed the room he bethought him of a garden of lilies; though why, for the life of him, he could not have explained. He heard his name mentioned, and saw the girl incline her head, but he made little, if any, acknowledgment; he stood quite still, looking at her and through her, and over her and beyond. For some moments he neither moved nor spoke. He was unconscious even that other guests had come.

He gave his hand absently to a popular novelist, Mr. A. B. Fenwick Chisholm-Jones by name, more familiarly known as Alphabet, whom Weldon brought to him, and kept his eyes on the yellow bodice. A fair young woman in pink had taken a position near to where he stood, and was complaining to someone that she had been obliged to give up cigarettes. And when the someone asked whether the abandonment of that pleasure was due to parental interference, the young woman laughed shortly, and explained that she was in training for a tennis tournament. Meanwhile the little group in which Tristrem stood was re-enforced by a new-comer, who attempted to condole with the novelist on the subject of an excoriating attack that one of the critics had recently made on his books, and suggested that he ought to do something about it. But of condolence or advice Mr. Jones would have none.

"Bah!" he exclaimed, "if the beggar doesn't like what I write let him try and do better. I don't care what any of them say. My books sell, and that's the *hauptsache*. Besides, what's the use in arguing with a newspaper? It's like talking metaphysics to a bull; the first you know, you get a horn in your navel." And while the novelist was expressing his disdain of all adverse criticism, and quoting Emerson to the effect that the average reviewer had the eyes of a bug and the heart of a cat, Tristrem discovered Mrs. Weldon's arm in his own, and presently found himself seated next to her at table.

At the extreme end, to the right of the host, was the girl with the amber eyes. The novelist was at her side. Evidently he had said something amusing, for they were both laughing; he with the complacency of one who has said a good thing, and she with the appreciation of one accustomed to wit. But Tristrem was not permitted to watch her undisturbed. Mrs. Weldon had a right to his attention, and she exercised that right with the pertinacity of a fly that has to be killed to be got rid of. "What do you think of Miss Finch?" she asked, with her stealthy giggle.

"Her name isn't Finch," Tristrem answered, indignantly.

"Yes it is, too—Flossy Finch, her name is; as if I oughtn't to know! Why, we were at Mrs. Garret and Mlle. de l'Entresol's school together for years and years. What makes you say her name isn't Finch? I had you here on purpose to meet her. Did you ever see such hair? There's only one girl in New York——"

"It *is* black," Tristrem assented.

"Black! Why, you must be crazy; it's orange, and that dress of hers——"

Tristrem looked down the table and saw a young lady whom he had not noticed before. Her hair, as Mrs. Weldon had said, was indeed the color of orange, though of an orange not over-ripe. "I thought you meant that girl next to Royal," he said.

"That! Oh! that's Miss Raritan."

Mrs. Weldon's voice had changed. Evidently Miss Raritan did not arouse in her the same enthusiasm as did Miss Finch. For a moment her lips lost their chromo smile, but presently it returned again, and she piped away anew on the subject of the charms of Flossy Finch, and after an interlude, of which Tristrem heard not one word, she turned and cross-questioned the man on her left.

The conversation had become very animated. From Royal's end of the table came intermittent shrieks of laughter. The novelist was evidently in his finest form. "Do you mean to tell me," Miss Finch asked him across the table, "do you mean to say that you don't believe in platonic affection?"

"I never uttered such a heresy in my life," the novelist replied. "Of course I believe in it; I believe in it thoroughly—between husband and wife."

At this everyone laughed again, except Tristrem, who had not heard, and Mrs. Weldon, who had not understood. The latter, however, felt that Miss Finch was distinguishing herself, and she turned to Tristrem anew.

"I want you to make yourself very agreeable to her," she said. "She is just the girl for you. Don't you think so? Now promise that you will talk to her after dinner."

"Talk metaphysics to a bull, and the first thing you know—the first thing you know—I beg your pardon, Mrs. Weldon, I didn't mean to say that—I don't know how the stupid phrase got in my head or why I said it." He hesitated a moment, and seemed to think. "H'm," he went on, "I am a trifle tired, I fancy."

Mrs. Weldon looked suspiciously at the glasses at his side, but apparently they had not been so much as tasted; they were full to the rim. She turned again to the guest at her left. The dinner was almost done. She asked a few more questions, and then presently, in a general lull, she gave a glance about her. At that signal the women-folk rose in a body, the men rising also, to let them pass.

Tristrem had risen mechanically with the others, and when the ultimate flounce had disappeared he sat down again and busied himself with a cup of coffee. The other men had drawn their chairs together near him, and over the liqueurs were discussing topics of masculine interest and flavor. Tristrem was about to make some effort to join in the conversation, when from beyond there came the running scale that is the prelude to the cabaletta, *Non più mesta*, from Cenerentola. Then, abruptly, a voice rang out as though it vibrated through labyrinths of gold—a voice that charged the air with resonant accords—a voice prodigious and dominating, grave and fluid; a voice that descended into the caverns of sound, soared to the uttermost heights, scattering notes like showers of stars, evoking visions of flesh and dazzling steel, and in its precipitate flights and vertiginous descents disclosing landscapes riotous with flowers, rich with perfume, sentient with beauty, articulate with love; a voice voluptuous as an organ and languorous as the consonance of citherns and guitars.

Tristrem, as one led in leash, moved from the table and passed into the outer room. Miss Raritan was at the piano. Beyond, a group of women sat hushed and mute; and still the resilient waves of song continued. One by one the men issued noiselessly from the inner room. And then, soon, the voice sank and died away like a chorus entering a crypt.

Miss Raritan rose from the piano. As she did so, Weldon, as it becomes a host, hastened to her. There was a confused hum, a murmur of applause, and above it rose a discreet and prolonged *brava* that must have come from the novelist. Weldon, seemingly, was urging her to sing again. The women had taken up anew some broken thread of gossip, but the men were at the piano, insisting too. Presently Miss Raritan resumed her seat, and the men moved back. Her fingers rippled over the keys like rain. She stayed them a second, and then, in a voice so low that it seemed hardly human, and yet so insistent that it would have filled a cathedral and scaled the dome, she began a ballad that breathed of Provence:

"O Magali, ma bien aimée,Fuyons tous deux sous la raméeAu fond du bois silencieux...."

When she had finished, Tristrem started. The earliest notes had sent the blood pulsing through his veins, thrilling him from finger-tips to the end of the spine, and then a lethargy enveloped him and he ceased to hear, and it was not until Miss Raritan stood up again from the piano that he was conscious that he had not been listening. He had sat near the entrance to the dining-room, and when the applause began afresh he passed out into the hall, found his coat and hat, and left the house.

As he walked down Irving Place he fell to wondering who it was that he had heard complain of being obliged to give up cigarettes, not on account of parental interference but because of a tournament. Yet, after all, what matter did it make? Certainly, he told himself, the Weldons seemed to live very well. Royal must be making money. Mrs. Weldon—Nanny, as Royal called her—was a nice little thing, somewhat—h'm, somewhat—well, not quite up to Royal. She looked like that girl in Munich, the girl that lived over the way, only Mrs. Weldon was prettier and dressed better, much better. Du hast die schönsten Augen. Munich wasn't a bad place, but what a hole Innsprück was. There was that Victoria Cross fellow; whatever became of him? He drank like a fish; it must have caught him by this time. H'm, he *would* give me the address of his shoemaker. I ought to have taken more from that man in Paris. Odd that the Cenerentola was the last thing I should have heard there. The buffo was good, so was the contralto. *She* sings much better. What a voice!

what a voice! Now, which was the more perfect, the voice or the girl? Let me see, which is the better fulfilled, the odor of the lily or the lily itself? Tulips I never cared for.... That is it, then. I wonder, though——

Tristrem had reached the house in Waverley Place. He let himself in with a latch-key, and went to his room. There he sat a while, companioned only by his thoughts. Before he fell asleep, his patriotism was riveted. A land that could produce such a specimen of girlhood outvalued Europe, Asia, and Africa combined—aye, a thousand times—and topped and exceeded creation.

III.

Among the effects and symptoms of love, there is an involuntary action of the mind which, since the days of Stendhal, has been known as crystallization. When a man becomes interested in a woman, when he pictures her not as she really is, but as she seems to him—as she ought to be, in fact—he experiences, first, admiration; second, desire; third, hope; and, behold, love or its counterfeit is born.

This crystallization affects the individual according to his nature. If that nature be inexperienced, unworn—in a word, if it be virginal, its earliest effects are those of a malady. On the other hand, if the nature on which it operates has received the baptism of fire, its effect is that of a tonic. To the one it is a fever, to the other a bugle-call. In the first instance, admiration is pursued by self-depreciation, desire is pinioned before conventional obstacles, and hope falters beneath a weight of doubt. In the second, admiration, desire, and hope are fused into one sentiment, the charm of the chase, the delight of the prospective quarry. As an example, there is Werther, and there is also Don Juan.

Now Tristrem Varick had never known a mother, sisters he had none, the feminine had been absent from his life, but in his nature there was an untarnishable refinement. During his student-days at Harvard, and throughout his residence abroad, there had been nothing of that which the French have agreed to denominate as *bonnes fortunes*. Such things may have been in his path, waiting only to be gathered, but, in that case, certain it is that he had passed them by unheeded. To use the figurative phrase, he was incapable of stretching his hand to any woman who had not the power of awakening a lasting affection; and during his wanderings, and despite, too, the example and easy morals of his comrades, no such woman having crossed his horizon, he had been innocent of even the most fugitive liaison. Nevertheless, the morning after the dinner in Gramercy Park, crystallization had done its work. He awoke with the surprise and wonder of an inexperienced sensation; he awoke with the consciousness of being in love, wholly, turbulently, absurdly in love with a girl to whom he had not addressed a single word.

The general opinion to the contrary notwithstanding, there are, after all, very few people who know what love really is. And among those that know, fewer there are that tell. A lexicographer, deservedly forgotten, has defined it as an exchange of fancies, the contact of two epiderms. Another, wiser if less epigrammatic, announced it as a something that no one knew what, coming no one knew whence, and ending no one knew how. But in whatever fashion it may be described, one thing is certain, it has been largely over-rated.

In the case of Tristrem Varick it appeared in its most perfect form. The superlative is used advisedly. Love has a hundred aspects, a thousand toilets. It may come at first sight, in which event, if it be enduring, it is, as Balzac has put it, a resultant of that prescience which is known as second sight. Or, it may come of the gradual fusion of two natures. It may come of propinquity, of curiosity, of sympathy, of hatred. It may come of the tremors of adolescence, the mutual attraction of one sex for the other; and, again, it may come of natural selection, of the discernment which leads a man through mazes of women to one in particular, to the woman who to him is the one woman in the world and manacles him at her feet. If Tristrem Varick had not met Miss Raritan, it is more than probable that he never would have known the meaning of the word.

When the first surprise at the discovery waned, delight took its place. He saw her amber eyes, he recalled as she had crossed the room the indolent undulation of her hips, he breathed the atmosphere of health which she exhaled, and in his ears her voice still rang. The *Non più mesta* of her song seemed almost a promise, and the *O Magali* an invitation. He recalled the movement of her lips, and fell to wondering what her name might be. At first he fancied that it might be Stella; but that, for some occult reason which only a lover would understand, he abandoned for Thyra, a name which pleasured him awhile and which he repeated aloud until it became sonorous as were it set in titles. But presently some defect presented itself, it sounded less apt, more suited to a blue-eyed daughter of a viking than to one so *brune* as she. Decidedly, Thyra did not suit her. And yet her name might be something utterly commonplace, such as Fanny, for instance, or Agnes, or Gertrude. But that was a possibility which he declined to entertain. When a girl is baptized, the mother, in choosing the name, should, he told himself, think of the lover who will one day pronounce it. And what had her mother chosen? It would be forethought indeed if she had selected Undine or even Iseult; but what mother was ever clairvoyant enough for that?

He thought this over awhile and was about to give the query up, when suddenly, without an effort on his part, he was visited by a name that announced her as the perfume announces the rose, a name that pictured and painted her, a name that suited her as did her gown of canary, a name that crowned her beauty and explained the melancholy of her lips. "It is Madeleine," he said, "it can be nothing else."

And into the syllables he threw the waving inflection of the French.

"It is Madeleine," he continued, "and when I see her I will tell in what way I divined it."

The possibility that she might be indifferent to such homage did not, for the moment, occur to him. He was loitering in the enchanted gardens of the imagination, which have been visited by us all. It was the improbable that fluttered his pulse.

Hitherto the life of Tristrem Varick had been that of a dilettante. There had been no reason why he should work. His education had unfitted him for labor, and his tastes, if artistic, were not sufficiently pronounced to act as incentives. He handled the brush well enough to know that he could never be a painter; he had a natural understanding of music, its value was clear to him, yet its composition was barred. The one talent that he possessed—a talent that grows rarer with the days—was that of appreciation, he could admire the masterpieces of others, but creation was not his. A few centuries ago he would have made an admirable knight-errant. In a material age like our own, his *raison a'être* was not obvious. In a word, he was just such an one as his father had intended he should be, one whose normal condition was that of chronic pluperfect subjunctive, and who, if thrown on his own resources, would be helpless indeed.

In some dim way he had been conscious of this before, and hitherto he had accepted it, as he had accepted his father's attitude, as one accepts the inevitable, and put it aside again as something against which, like death, or like life, it is useless to rebel. After all, there was nothing particularly dreadful about it. An inability to be Somebody was not a matter of which the District Attorney is obliged to take cognizance. At least he need do no harm, and he would have wealth enough to do much good. It was in thoughts like these that hitherto he had found consolation. But on this particular morning he looked for them anew, and the search was fruitless. Not one of the old consolations disclosed the slightest worth. He stood before himself naked in his nothingness. The true knowledge of his incompetence had never come home to him before—but now it closed round him in serried arguments, and in the closing shut out all hope of her. Who was he, indeed, to pretend to such a girl?

To win her, he told himself, one must needs be a conqueror, one who has coped with dangers and could flaunt new triumphs as his lady's due. Some soldier bearing a marshal's baton back from war, some hero that had liberated an empire or stolen a republic for himself, some prince of literature or satrap of song, someone, in fact, who, booted and spurred, had entered the Temple of Fame, and claimed the dome as his. But he! What had he to offer? His name, however historical and respected, was an accident of birth. Of the wealth which he would one day possess he had not earned a groat. And, were it lost, the quadrature of the circle would not be more difficult than its restoration. And yet, and yet—though any man she could meet might be better and wiser and stronger than he, not one would care for her more. At least there was something in that, a tangible value, if ever there were one. There was every reason why she should turn her back, and that one reason, and that one only, why she should not. But that one reason, he told himself, was a force in itself. The resuscitation of hope was so sudden that the blood mounted to his temples and pulsated through his veins.

He left the bed in which his meditations had been passed. "They say everything comes to him who waits," he muttered, and then proceeded to dress. He took a tub and got himself, absent-mindedly, into a morning suit. "I don't believe it," he exclaimed, at last, "the world belongs to the impatient, and I am impatient of her."

Tristrem was in no sense a diplomatist. In his ways there was a candor that was as unusual as it is delightful; yet such is the power of love that, in its first assault, the victim is transformed. The miser turns prodigal, the coward brave, the genius becomes a simpleton, and in the simpleton there awakes a Machiavelli. Tristrem passed a forenoon in trying to unravel as cruel a problem as has ever been given a lover to solve—how, in a city like New York, to meet a girl of whom he knew absolutely nothing, and who was probably unaware of his own existence. He might have waited, it is true—chance holds many an odd trick—but he had decided to be impatient, and in his impatience he went to Gramercy Park and drank tea there, not once, but four afternoons in succession, an excess of civility which surprised Mrs. Weldon not a little.

That he should make an early visit of digestion was quite in the order of things, but when that visit was repeated again and again, Mrs. Weldon, with a commingling of complacency and alarm, told herself that, in her quality of married woman, such persistence should be discouraged. But the opportunity for such discouragement did not present itself, or rather, when it did the need of discouragement had passed. Tristrem drank tea with her several times, and then disappeared abruptly. "He must have known it was hopeless," she reflected, when a week went by unmarked by further enterprise on his part. And then, the intended discouragement notwithstanding, she felt vaguely vexed.

In the tea-drinking Tristrem's object, if not apparent to Mrs. Weldon, was perfectly clear to himself. He desired to learn something of Miss Raritan, and he knew, if the tea-drinking was continued with sufficient endurance, not only would he acquire, from a talkative lady like his hostess, information of the amplest kind, which after all was secondary, but that in the course of a week the girl herself must put in an appearance. A dinner call, if not obligatory to him, was obligatory to her, and on that obligation he counted.

To those who agree to be bound by what the Western press calls etiquette, there is nothing more inexorable than a social debt. A woman may contest her mantua-maker's bill with impunity, her antenuptial promises may go to protest and she remain unstopped; but let her leave a dinner-call overdue and unpaid, then is she shameless indeed. In this code Tristrem was necessarily learned. On returning to Fifth Avenue he had marvelled somewhat at noting that laws which applied to one sex did not always extend to the other, that civility was not exacted of men, that politeness was relegated to the tape-counter and out of place in a drawing-room; in a word, that it was not good form to be courteous, and not ill-bred to be rude.

While the tea-drinking was in progress he managed without much difficulty to get Mrs. Weldon on the desired topic. There were spacious digressions in her information and abrupt excursions into irrelevant matter, and there were also interruptions by other visitors, and the consequent and tedious exchange of platitude and small-talk. But after the fourth visit Tristrem found himself in possession of a store of knowledge, the sum and substance of which amounted to this: Miss Raritan lived with her mother in the shady part of the Thirties, near Madison Avenue. Her father was dead. It had been rumored, but with what truth Mrs. Weldon was not prepared to affirm, that the girl had some intention of appearing on the lyric stage, which, if she carried out, would of course be the end of her socially. She had been very much ruin after on account of her voice, and at the Wainwarings the President had said that he had never heard anything like it, and asked her to come to Washington and be present at one of the diplomatic dinners. Personally Mrs. Weldon knew her very slightly, but she intimated that, inasmuch as the government had once sent Raritan *père* abroad as minister—in order probably to be rid of him—his daughter was inclined to look down on those whose fathers held less exalted positions—on Mrs. Weldon herself, for example.

It was with this little store of information that Tristrem left her on the Thursday succeeding the dinner. It was meagre indeed, and yet ample enough to afford him food for reflection. During the gleaning many people had come and gone, but of Miss Raritan he had as yet seen nothing. The next afternoon, however, as he was about to ascend Mrs. Weldon's stoop for the fifth time in five days, the door opened and the girl on whom his thoughts were centred was before him.

Throughout the week he had lived in the expectation of meeting her, it was the one thing that had brought zest to the day and dreams to the night; there was even a little speech which he had rehearsed, but for the moment he was dumb. He plucked absently at his cuff, to the palms of his hands there came a sudden moisture. In the vestibule above, a servant stood waiting for Miss Raritan to reach the pavement before closing the door, and abruptly, from a barrel-organ at the corner, a waltz was thrown out in jolts.

The girl descended the steps before Tristrem was able to master his emotion.

"Miss Raritan," he began, hastily, "I don't suppose you remember me. I am Mr. Varick. I heard you sing the other night. I have come here every day since in the hope of——; you see, I wanted to ask if I might not have the privilege of hearing you sing again?"

"If you consider it a privilege, certainly. On Sunday evening, though, I thought you seemed rather bored." She made this answer very graciously, with her head held like a bird's, a trifle to one side.

Tristrem gazed at her in a manner that would have mollified a tigress. "I was not bored. I had never heard anyone sing before."

"Yet your friend, Mr. Weldon, tells me that you are very fond of music."

"That is exactly what I mean."

At this speech of his she looked at him, musingly. "I wish I deserved that," she said.

Tristrem began again with new courage. "It is like anything else, I fancy. I doubt if anyone, ignorant of difficulties overcome, ever appreciates a masterpiece. A sonnet, if perfect, is only perfect to a sonneteer. The gallery may applaud a drama, it is the playwright who judges it at its worth. It is the sculptor that appreciates a Canova——"

They had reached the corner where the barrel-organ was in ambush. A woman dragging a child with Italy and dirt in its face followed them, her hand outstretched. Tristrem had an artful way of being rid of a beggar, and after the fumble of a moment he gave her some coin.

"—And the artist who appreciates rags," added Miss Raritan.

"Perhaps. I am not fond of rags myself, but I have often caught myself envying the simplicity which they sometimes conceal. That woman, now, she may be as pleased with my little gift as I am to be walking with you."

"I thought it was my voice you liked," Miss Raritan answered, demurely.

Tristrem experienced a mental start. A suspicion entered his mind which he chased indignantly. There was about the girl an aroma that was incompatible with coquetry.

"You would not, I am sure, have me think of you in the *vox et præterea nihil* style," he replied. "To be candid, I thought that very matter over the other night." He hesitated, as though waiting for some question, but she did not so much as look at him, and he continued unassisted. "I thought of a flower and its perfume, I wondered which was the more admirable, and—and—I decided that I did not care for tulips."

"But that you did care for me, I suppose?"

"Yes, I decided that."

Miss Raritan threw back her head with a movement indicative of impatience.

"I didn't mean to tell you," he added—"that is, not yet."

They had crossed Broadway and were entering Fifth Avenue. There the stream of carriages kept them a moment on the curb.

"I hope," Tristrem began again, "I hope you are not vexed."

"Vexed at what? No, I am not vexed. I am tired; every other man I meet— There, we can cross now. Besides, I am married. Don't get run over. I am going in that shop."

"You are *not* married!"

"Yes, I am; if I were a Harvard graduate I would say to Euterpe. As it is, Scales is more definite." She had led him to the door of a milliner, a portal which Tristrem knew was closed to him. "If you care to come and see me," she added, by way of *congé*, "my husband will probably be at home." And with that she opened the door and passed into the shop.

"I can imagine a husband," thought Tristrem, with a glimmer of that spirit of belated repartee which Thackeray called cab-wit, the brilliancy which comes to us when we are going home, "I can imagine a husband whose greatest merit is his wife."

IV.

The fact that few days elapsed before Tristrem Varick availed himself of Miss Raritan's invitation, and that thereafter he continued to avail himself of it with frequence and constancy, should surprise no one. During the earliest of these visits he met Miss Raritan's mother, and was unaccountably annoyed when he heard that lady address her daughter as Viola. He had been so sure that her baptismal name was Madeleine that the one by which he found she was called sounded false as an alias, and continued so to sound until he accustomed himself to the syllables and ended by preferring it to the Madeleine of his fancy. This, however, by the way. Mrs. Raritan was a woman who, in her youth, must have been very beautiful, and traces of that beauty she still preserved. When she spoke her voice endeared her to you, and in her manner there was that something which made you feel that she might be calumniated, as good women often are, but yet that she could never be the subject of gossip. She did not seem resolute, but she did seem warm of heart, and Tristrem felt at ease with her at once.

Of her he saw at first but little. In a city like New York it is difficult for anyone to become suddenly intimate in a household, however cordial and well-intentioned that household may be. And during those hours of the winter days when Miss Raritan was at home it was seldom that her mother was visible. But it was not long before Tristrem became an occasional guest at dinner, and it was in the process of breaking bread that a semblance of intimacy was established. And at last, when winter had gone and the green afternoons opposed the dusk, Tristrem now and then would drop in of an evening, and in the absence of Miss Raritan pass an hour with her mother. Truly she was not the rose, but did she not dwell at her side?

Meanwhile, Miss Raritan's attitude differed but little from the one which she had first adopted. She treated Tristrem with exasperating familiarity, and kept him at arm's length. She declined to see him when the seeing would have been easy, and summoned him when the summons was least to be expected. He was useful to her as a piece of furniture, and she utilized him as such. In the matter of flowers and theatres he was a convenience. And at routs and assemblies the attention of an heir apparent to seven million was a homage and a tribute which Miss Raritan saw no reason to forego.

In this Tristrem had no one but himself to blame. He had been, and was, almost canine in his demeanor to her. She saw it, knew it, felt it, and treated him accordingly. And he, with the cowardice of love, made little effort at revolt. Now and then he protested to Mrs. Raritan, to whom he had made no secret of his admiration for her daughter, and who consoled him as best she might; but that was all. And so the winter passed and the green afternoons turned sultry, and Tristrem was not a step further advanced than on the day when he had left the girl at the milliner's. On the infrequent occasions when he had ventured to say some word of that which was nearest his heart, she had listened with tantalizing composure, and when he had paused for encouragement or rebuke, she would make a remark of such inappositeness that anyone else would have planted her there and gone. But Tristrem was none other than himself; his nature commanded and he obeyed.

It so happened that one May morning a note was brought him, in which Miss Raritan said that her mother and herself were to leave in a day or two for the country, and could he not get her something to read on the way. Tristrem passed an hour selecting, with infinite and affectionate care, a small bundle of foreign literature. In the package he found room for Balzac's "Pierrette" and the "Curé de Tours," one of Mme. Craven's stupidities, a volume of platitude in rhyme by François Coppée, a copy of De Amicis' futile wanderings in Spain—a few samples, in fact, of the *pueris virginibusque* school. And that evening, with the bundle under his arm, he sought Miss Raritan.

The girl glanced at the titles and put the books aside. "When we get in order at Narragansett," she said, "I wish you would come up."

Had she kissed him, Tristrem could not have revelled more. "There are any number of hotels," she added, by way of douche.

"Certainly, if you wish it, but—but———"

"Well, but what?"

"I don't know. You see—well, it's this way: You know that I love you, and you know also that you care for me as for the snows of yester-year. There is no reason why you should do otherwise. I don't mean to complain. If I am unable to make you care, the fault is mine. I did think—h'm—no matter. What I wanted to say is this: there is no reason why you should care, and yet———. See here; take two slips of paper, write on one, I will marry you, and, on the other, Put a bullet through your head, and let me draw. I would take the chance so gladly. But that chance, of course, you will not give. Why should you, after all? Why should I give everything I own to the first beggar I meet? But why should you have any other feeling for me than that which you have? And yet, sometimes I think you don't understand. Any man you meet could be more attractive than I, and very easy he would find it to be so; but no one could care for you more—no one———"

Miss Raritan was sitting opposite to him, her feet crossed, her head thrown back, her eyes fixed on the ceiling. One arm lay along the back of the lounge which she occupied, the other was pendant at her side. And while he still addressed her, she arose with the indolence of a panther, crossed the room, picked up a miniature from a table, eyed it as though she had never seen it before and did not particularly care to see it again, and then, seating herself at the piano, she attacked the *Il segreto per esser felice*, the brindisi from "Lucrezia Borgia."

In the wonder of her voice Tristrem forgot the discourtesy of the action. He listened devoutly. And, as he listened, each note was an electric shock. *Il segreto per esser felice*, indeed! The secret of happiness was one which she alone of all others in the world could impart. And, as the measures of the song rose and fell, they brought him a transient exhilaration like to that which comes of champagne, dowering him with factitious force wherewith to strive anew. And so it happened that, when the ultimate note had rung out and the girl's fingers loitered on the keys, he went over to her with a face so eloquent that she needed but a glance at it to know what he was seeking to say.

With a gesture coercive as a bit, she lifted one hand from the keys and stayed his lips. Then, she stood up and faced him. "Tristrem," she began, "when I first saw you I told you that I was married to my art. And in an art such as mine there is no divorce. It may be that I shall go on the stage. After all, why should I not? Is society so alluring that I should sacrifice for it that which is to me infinitely preferable? If I have not done so already it is because of my mother. But should I decide to do so, there are years of study before me yet. In which case I could not marry, that is self-evident, not only because I would not marry a man who would suffer me to sing in public—don't interrupt—but also because—well, you told me that you understood the possibilities of the human voice, and you must know what the result would be. But even independent of that, you said a moment ago that I did not love you. Well, I don't. I don't love you. Tristrem, listen to me. I don't love you as you would have me. I wish I did. But I like you. I like you as I can like few other men. Tristrem, except my mother, I have not a friend in the world. Women never care for me, and men—well, save in the case of yourself, when their friendship has been worth the having, it belonged to someone else. Give me yours."

"It will be hard, very hard."

Miss Raritan moved from where she had been standing and glanced at the clock. "You must go now," she said, "but promise that you will try."

She held her hand to him, and Tristrem raised it to his lips and kissed the wrist. "You might as well ask me to increase my stature," he answered. And presently he dropped the hand which he held and left the house.

It was a perfect night. The moon hung like a yellow feather in the sky, and in the air was a balm that might have come from fields of tamaris and of thyme. The street itself was quiet, and as Tristrem walked on, something of the enchantment of the hour fell upon him. On leaving Miss Raritan, he had been irritated at himself. It seemed to him that when with her he was at his worst; that he stood before her dumb for love, awkward, embarrassed, and ineffectual of speech. It seemed to him that he lacked the tact of other men, and that, could she see him as he really was when unemotionalized by her presence, if the eloquence which came to him in solitude would visit him once at her side, if he could plead to her with the fervor with which he addressed the walls, full surely her answer would be other. She would make no proffer then of friendship, or if she did, it would be of that friendship which is born of love, and is better than love itself. But as he walked on the enchantment of the night encircled him. He declined to accept her reply; he told himself that in his eagerness he had been abrupt; that a girl who was worth the winning was slow of capture; that he had expected months to give him what only years could afford, and that Time, in which all things unroll, might yet hold this gift for him. He resolved to put his impatience aside like an unbecoming coat. He would pretend to be but a friend. As a friend he would be privileged to see her, and then, some day the force and persistence of his affection would do the rest. He smiled at his own cunning. It was puerile as a jack-straw, but it seemed shrewdness itself to him. Yes, that was the way. He had done wrong; he had unmasked his batteries too soon. And such batteries! But no matter, of his patience he was now assured. On the morrow he would go to her and begin the campaign anew.

He had reached the corner and was on the point of turning down the avenue, when a hansom rattled up and wheeled so suddenly into the street through which he had come, that he stepped back a little to let it pass. As he did so he looked in at the fare. The cab was beyond him in a second, but in the momentary glimpse which he caught of the occupant, he recognized Royal Weldon. And as he continued his way, he wondered where Royal Weldon could be going.

The following evening he went to dine at the Athenæum Club. The house in Waverley Place affected him as might an empty bier in a tomb. The bread that he broke there choked him. His father was as congenial as a spectre. He only appeared when dinner was announced, and after he had seated himself at the table he asked grace of God in a low, determined fashion, and that was the end of the conversation. Tristrem remembered that in the infrequent vacations of his school and college days, that was the way it always had been, and being tolerably convinced that that was the way it always would be, he preferred, when not expected elsewhere, to dine at the club.

On entering the Athenæum on this particular evening, he put his hat and coat in the vestiary and was about to order dinner, when he was accosted by Alphabet Jones.

"I say, Varick," the novelist exclaimed—(during the winter they had seen much of each other), "do you know who was the originator of the cloakroom? Of course you don't—I'll tell you; who do you suppose now? Give it up? Mrs. Potiphar! How's that? Good enough for Theodore Hook, eh? Let's dine together, and I'll tell you some more."

"Let's dine together" was a formula which Mr. Jones had adopted. Literally, it meant, I'll order and you pay. Tristrem was aware in what light the invitation should be viewed, he had heard it before; but, though the novelist was of the genus *spongia*, he was seldom tiresome, often entertaining, and moreover, Tristrem was one who would rather pay than not. As there were few of that category in the club, Mr. Jones made a special prey of him, and on this particular evening, when the ordering had been done and the dinner announced, he led him in triumph to the lift.

As they were about to step in, Weldon stepped out. He seemed hurried and would have passed on with a nod, but Tristrem caught him by the arm. Of late he had seen little of him, and it had seemed to Tristrem that the fault, if fault there were, must be his own.

"I caught a glimpse of you last night, didn't I, Royal?" he asked.

Weldon raised his eyebrows for all response. Evidently he was not in a conversational mood. But at once an idea seemed to strike him. "I dare say," he answered, "I roam about now and then like anyone else. By the way, where are you going to-night? Why not look in on my wife? She says you neglect her."

"I would like it, Royal, but the fact is I am going to make a call."

"In Thirty-ninth Street?"

Tristrem looked at him much as a yokel at a fair might look at a wizard. He was so astonished at Weldon's prescience that he merely nodded.

"You can save yourself the trouble then—I happened to meet Miss Raritan this afternoon. She is dining at the Wainwarings. Look in at Gramercy Park." And with that he turned on his heel and disappeared into the smoking-room.

"Didn't I hear Weldon mention Miss Raritan?" Jones asked, when he and Tristrem had finished the roast. "There's a girl I'd like to put in a book. She has hell in her eyes and heaven in her voice. What a heroine she would make!" he exclaimed, enthusiastically; and then in a complete change of key, in a tone that was pregnant with suggestion, he added, "and what a wife!"

"I don't understand you," said Tristrem, in a manner which, for him, was defiant.

Whether or not Jones was a good sailor is a matter of small moment. In any event he tacked at once.

"Bah! I am speaking in the first person. I don't believe in matrimony myself, I am too poor. And besides, I never heard of but one happy marriage, and that was between a blind man and a deaf-mute. Though even then it must have been difficult to know what the woman thought. Now, in regard to Miss Raritan, half the men in the city are after her, *pour le bon motif, s'entend*; but when a girl has had the *dessus du panier* at her feet, no fellow can afford to ask her to take a promenade with him down the aisle of Grace Church, unless he has the Chemical Bank in one pocket and the United States Trust Company in the other. *Et avec ça!*" And Jones waved his head as though not over-sure that the coffers of those institutions would suffice.

"I don't see what that has to do with it," Tristrem indignantly interjected.

"Isn't that odd now?" was Jones' sarcastic reply. "Dr. Holmes says that no fellow can be a thorough-going swell unless he has three generations in oil. And mind you, daguerreotypes won't do. There are any number of your ancestors strung along the walls of the Historical Society, and how many more you may have in that crypt of yours in Waverley Place, heaven only knows. Imprimis, if you accept Dr. Holmes as an authority, you are a thorough-going swell. In the second place, you look like a Greek shepherd. Third, you are the biggest catch in polite society. Certainly it's odd that with such possibilities you should see no reason for not marrying a girl who will want higher-stepping horses than Elisha's, and who, while there is a bandit of a dressmaker in Paris, will decline to imitate the lilies of the field. Certainly——"

"I never said anything about it, I never said anything about marrying or not marrying——"

"Oh, didn't you? I thought you did." And Jones leaned back in his chair and summoned a waiter with an upward movement of the chin. "Bring another pint of this, will you."

"I think I won't take anything more," said Tristrem, rising from the table as he spoke. "It's hot in here. I may see you down-stairs." And with that he left the room.

Mr. Alphabet Jones looked after him a second and nodded sagaciously to himself. "Another man overboard," he muttered, as he toyed with his empty glass. "*Ah! jeunesse, jeunesse!*"

V.

Tristrem descended the stair and hesitated a moment at the door of the smoking-room. Near-by, at a small table, two men were drinking brandy. He caught a fragment of their speech: it was about a woman. Beyond, another group was listening to that story of the eternal feminine which is everlastingly the same. Within, the air was lifeless and heavy with the odor of cigars, but in the hall there came through the wide portals of the entrance the irresistible breath of a night in May.

Tristrem turned and presently sauntered aimlessly out of the club and up the avenue. Before him, a man was loitering with a girl; his arm was in hers, and he was whispering in her ear. A cab passed, bearing a couple that sat waist-encircled devouring each other with insatiate eyes. And at Twenty-third Street, a few shop-girls, young and very pretty, that were laughing conspicuously together, were joined by some clerks, with whom they paired off and disappeared. At the corner, through the intersecting thoroughfares came couple after couple, silent for the most part, as though oppressed by the invitations of the night. Beyond, in the shadows of the Square, the benches were filled with youths and maidens, who sat hand-in-hand, oblivious to the crowd that circled in indolent coils about them. The moon had not yet risen, but a leash of stars that night had loosed glowed and trembled with desire. The air was sentient with murmurs, redolent with promise. The avenues and the adjacent streets seemed to have forgotten their toil and to swoon unhushed in the bewitchments of a dream of love.

Tristrem found himself straying through its mazes and convolutions. Whichever way he turned there was some monition of its presence. From a street-car which had stayed his passage he saw the conductor blow a kiss to a hurrying form, and through an open window of Delmonico's he saw a girl with summer in her eyes reach across the table at which she sat and give her companion's hand an abrupt yet deliberate caress.

Tristrem continued his way, oppressed. He was beset by an insidious duscholia. He felt as one does who witnesses a festival in which there is no part for him. The town reeked with love as a brewery reeks with beer. The stars, the air, the very pavements told of it. It was omnipresent, and yet there was none for him.

He tried to put it from him and think of other things. Of Jones, for instance. Why had he spoken of Viola? And then, in the flight of fancies which surged through his mind, there was one that he stayed and detained. It was that he must see her again before she left town. He looked at his watch: it lacked twenty minutes to ten, and on the impulse of the moment he hailed a passing 'bus. It was inexplicable to him that the night before she should have let him go without a word as to her movements. It seemed to be understood that he was to come again to wish her a pleasant journey. And when was he to come if not that very evening? Surely at the time she had forgotten this engagement with the Wainwarings, and some note had been left for him at the door. And if no note had been left, then why should he not ask for her mother or wait till she returned? A bell rang sharply through the vehicle and aroused him from his reverie. He glanced up, and saw the driver eyeing him through the machicoulis of glass. It was the fare he wanted, and as Tristrem deposited it in the box he noticed that the familiar street was reached.

In a few moments he was at the house. On the stoop a servant was occupied with the mat.

"Is, eh, did——"

"Yes, sir," the man answered, promptly. "Miss Raritan is in the parlor."

In the surprise at the unexpected, Tristrem left his hat and coat, and pushing aside the portière, he entered the room unannounced. At first he fancied that the servant had been mistaken. Miss Raritan was not at her accustomed place, and he stood at the door-way gazing about in uncertainty. But in an instant, echoing from the room beyond, he caught the sound of her voice; yet in the voice was a tone which he had never heard before—a tone of smothered anger that carried with it the accent of hate.

Moved by unconscious springs, he left the door-way and looked into the adjoining room. A man whom at first he did not recognize was standing by a lounge from which he had presumably arisen. And before him, with both her small hands clinched and pendent, and in her exquisite face an expression of relentless indignation, stood Miss Raritan. Another might have thought them rehearsing a tableau for some theatricals of the melodramatic order, but not Tristrem. He felt vaguely alarmed: there came to him that premonition without which no misfortune ever occurs; and suddenly the alarm changed to bewilderment. The man had turned: it was Royal Weldon. Tristrem could not credit his senses. He raised his hand to his head: it did not seem possible that a felon could have told a more wanton lie than he had been told but little over an hour before; and yet the teller of that lie was his nearest friend. And still he did not understand; surely there was some mistake. He would have spoken, but Weldon crossed the room to where he stood, and with set teeth and contracted muscles fronted him a second's space, and into his eyes he looked a defiance that was the more hideous in that it was mute. Then, with a gesture that almost tore the portière from its rings, he passed out into the hall and let the curtain fall behind him.

As he passed on Tristrem turned with the obedience of a subject under the influence of a mesmerist; and when the curtain fell again he started as subjects do when they awake from their trance.

The fairest, truest, and best may be stricken in the flush of health; yet after the grave has opened and closed again does not memory still subsist, and to the mourner may not the old dreams return? However acute the grief may be, is it not often better to know that affection is safe in the keeping of the dead than to feel it at the mercy of the living? We may prate as we will, but there are many things less endurable than the funeral of the best-beloved. Death is by no means the worst that can come. Whoso discovers that affection reposed has been given to an illusory representation; to one not as he is, but as fancy pictured him; to a trickster that has cheated the heart—in fact, to a phantom that has no real existence outside of the imagination, must experience a sinking more sickening than any corpse can convey. At the moment, the crack of doom that is to herald an eternal silence cannot more appal.

Tristrem still stood gazing at the portière through which Weldon had disappeared. He heard the front door close, and the sound of feet on the pavement. And presently he was back at St. Paul's, hurrying from the Upper School to intercede with the master. It was bitterly cold that morning, but in the afternoon the weather had moderated, and they had both gone to skate. And then the day he first came. He remembered his good looks, his patronizing, precocious ways; everything, even to the shirt he wore—blue, striped with white—and the watch with the crest and the motto *Well done, Weldon*. No, it was ill done, Weldon, and the lie was ignoble. And why had he told it? Their friendship, seemingly, had been so stanch, so unmarred by disagreement, that this lie was as a dash of blood on a white wall—an ineffaceable stain.

If there are years that count double, there are moments in which the hourglass is transfixed. The entire scene, from Tristrem's entrance to Weldon's departure, was compassed in less than a minute, yet during that fragment of time there had been enacted a drama in epitome—a drama humdrum and ordinary indeed, but in which Tristrem found himself bidding farewell to one whom he had never known.

He was broken in spirit, overwhelmed by the suddenness of the disaster, and presently, as though in search of sympathy, he turned to Miss Raritan. The girl had thrown herself in a chair, and sat, her face hidden in her hands. As Tristrem approached her she looked up. Her cheeks were blanched.

"He told me you were at the Wainwaring's," Tristrem began. "I don't see," he added, after a moment—"I don't understand why he should have done so. He knew you were here, yet he said——"

"Did you hear what he said to me?"

Tristrem for all response shook his head wonderingly.

The girl's cheeks from white had turned flame.

"He has not been to you the friend you think," she said, and raising her arm to her face, she made a gesture as though to brush from her some distasteful thing.

"But what has he done? What did he say?"

"Don't ask me. Don't mention him to me." She buried her face again in her hands and was silent.

Tristrem turned uneasily and walked into the other room, and then back again to where she sat; but still she hid her face and was silent. And Tristrem left her and continued his walk, this time to the dining-room and then back to the parlor which he had first entered. And after a while Miss Raritan stood up from her seat and as though impelled by the nervousness of her companion, she, too, began to pace the rooms, but in the contrary direction to that which Tristrem had chosen. At last she stopped, and when Tristrem approached her she beckoned him to her side.

"What did you say to me last night?" she asked.

"What did I say? I said—you asked me—I said it would be difficult."

"Do you think so still?"

"Always."

"Tristrem, I will be your wife."

A Cimmerian led out of darkness into sudden light could not marvel more at multicolored vistas than did Tristrem, at this promise. Truly they are most hopeless who have hoped the most. And Tristrem, as he paced the rooms, had told himself it was done. His hopes had scattered before him like last year's leaves. He had groped in shadows and had been conscious only of a blind alley, with a dead wall, somewhere, near at hand. But now, abruptly, the shadows had gone, the blind alley had changed into a radiant avenue, the dead wall had parted like a curtain, and beyond was a new horizon, gold-barred and blue, and landscapes of asphodels and beckoning palms. He was as one who, overtaken by sleep on the banks of the Styx, awakes in Arcadia.

His face was so eloquent with the bewitchments through which he roamed that, for the first time that evening, Miss Raritan smiled. She raised a finger warningly.

"Now, Tristrem, if you say anything ridiculous I will take it back."

But the warning was needless. Tristrem caught the finger, and kissed her hand with old-fashioned grace.

"Viola," he said, at last, "I thank you. I do not know what I can do to show how I appreciate this gift of gifts. But yet, if it is anything, if it can bring any happiness to a girl to know that she fills a heart to fulfilment itself, that she dwells in thought as the substance of thought, that she animates each fibre of another's being, that she enriches a life with living springs, and feels that it will be never otherwise, then you will be happy, for so you will always be to me."

The speech, if pardonably incoherent, was not awkwardly made, and it was delivered with a seriousness that befitted the occasion. In a tone as serious as his own, she answered:

"I will be true to you, Tristrem." That was all. But she looked in his face as she spoke.

They had been standing, but now they found seats near to each other. Tristrem would not release her hand, and she let it lie unrebellious in his own. And in this fashion they sat and mapped the chartless future. Had Tristrem been allowed his way the marriage would have been an immediate one. But to this, of course, Miss Raritan would not listen.

"Not before November," she said, with becoming decision.

"Why, that is five months off!"

"And months are short, and then——"

"But, Viola, think! Five months! It is a kalpa of time. And besides," he added, with the cogent egotism of an accepted lover, "what shall I do with myself in the meantime?"

"If you are good you may come to the Pier, and there we will talk edelweiss and myosotis, as all engaged people do." She said this so prettily that the sarcasm, if sarcasm there were, was lost.

To this programme Tristrem was obliged to subscribe.

"Well, then, afterward we will go abroad."

"Don't you like this country?" the girl asked, all the stars and stripes fluttering in her voice, and in a tone which one might use in reciting, "Breathes there the man, with soul so dead?"

"I think," he answered, apologetically, "that I do like this country. It is a great country. But New York is not a great city, at least not to my thinking. Collectively it is great, I admit, but individually not, and that is to me the precise difference between it and Paris. Collectively the French amount to little, individually it is otherwise."

"But you told me once that Paris was tiresome."

"I was not there with you. And should it become so when we are there together, we have the whole world to choose from. In Germany we can have the middle ages over again. In London we can get the flush of the nineteenth century. There is all of Italy, from the lakes to Naples. We can take a doge's palace in Venice, or a Cæsar's villa on the Baia. With a dahabieh we could float down into the dawn of history. You would look well in a dahabieh, Viola."

"As Aida?"

"Better. And that reminds me, Viola; tell me, you will give up all thought of the stage, will you not?"

"How foolish you are. Fancy Mrs. Tristrem Varick before the footlights. There are careers open to a girl that the acceptance of another's name must close. And the stage is one of them. I should have adopted it long ago, had it not been for mother. She seems to think that a Raritan—but there, you know what mothers are. Now, of course, I shall give it up. Besides, Italian opera is out of fashion. And even if it were otherwise, have I not now a lord, a master, whom I must obey?"

Her eyes looked anything but obedience, yet her voice was melodious with caresses.

And so they sat and talked and made their plans, until it was long past the conventional hour, and Tristrem felt that he should go. He had been afloat in unnavigated seas of happiness, but still in his heart he felt the burn of a red, round wound. The lie that Weldon had told smarted still, yet with serener spirit he thought there might be some unexplained excuse.

"Tell me," he asked, as he was about to leave, "what was it Weldon said?"

Miss Raritan looked at him, and hesitated before she spoke. Then catching his face in her two hands she drew it to her own.

"He said you were a goose," she whispered, and touched her lips to his.

With this answer Tristrem was fain to be content. And presently, when he left the house, he reeled as though he had drunk beaker after flagon of the headiest wine.

VI.

After a ten-mile pull on the river, a shandygaff of Bass and champagne is comforting to the oarsman. It is accounted pleasant to pay a patient creditor an outlawed debt. But a poet has held that the most pleasurable thing imaginable is to awake on a summer morning with the consciousness of being in love. Even in winter the sensation ought not to be disagreeable; yet when to the consciousness of being in love is added the belief that the love is returned, then the bleakest day of all the year must seem like a rose of June.

Tristrem passed the night in dreams that told of Her. He strayed through imperishable beauties, through dawns surrounded by candors of hope. The breath of brooks caressed him, he was enveloped in the sorceries of a sempiternal spring. The winds, articulate with song, choired to the skies ululations and messages of praise. Each vista held a promise. The horizon was a prayer fulfilled. He saw grief collapse and joy enthroned. From bird and blossom he caught the incommunicable words of love. And when from some new witchery he at last awoke, he smiled—the real was fairer than the dream.

For some time he loitered in the gardens which his fancy disclosed, spectacular-wise, for his own delight, until at last he bethought him of the new duties of his position and of the accompanying necessity of making those duties known to those to whom he was related. Then, after a breakfast of sliced oranges and coffee, he rang for the servant and told him to ask his father whether he could spare a moment that morning. In a few minutes the servant returned. "Mr. Varick will be happy to see you, sir," he said.

"What did he say?" Tristrem asked; "what were his exact words?"

"Well, sir, I said as how you presented your compliments, and could you see him, and he didn't say nothing; he was feeding the bird. But I could tell, sir; when Mr. Varick doesn't like a thing, he looks at you and if he does, he doesn't."

"And he didn't look at you?"

"No, sir, he didn't turn his 'ead."

"H'm," said Tristrem to himself, as he descended the stairs, "I wonder, when I tell him, whether he will look at me." And the memory of his father's stare cast a shadow on his buoyant spirits.

On entering the room in which Mr. Varick passed his mornings, Tristrem found that gentleman seated at a table. In one hand he held a bronze-colored magazine, and in the other a silver knife. In the window was a gilt cage in which a bird was singing, and on the table was a profusion of roses—the room itself was vast and chill. One wall was lined, the entire length, with well-filled book-shelves. In a corner was a square pile of volumes, bound in pale sheep, which a lawyer would have recognized as belonging to the pleasant literature of his profession. And over the book-shelves was a row of Varicks, standing in the upright idleness which is peculiar to portraits in oil. It was many years since Tristrem had entered this room; yet now, save for the scent of flowers and the bird-cage, it was practically unchanged.

"Father," he began at once, "I would not have ventured to disturb you if—if—that is, unless I had something important to say." He was looking at his father, but his father was not looking at him. "It is this," he continued, irritated in spite of himself by the complete disinterestedness of one whose son he was; "I am engaged to be married."

At this announcement Mr. Varick fluttered the paper-knife, but said nothing.

"The young lady is Miss Raritan," he added, and then paused, amazed at the expression of his father's face. It was as though unseen hands were torturing it at will. The mouth, cheeks, and eyelids quivered and twitched, and then abruptly Mr. Varick raised the bronze-colored magazine, held it before his tormented features, and when he lowered it again his expression was as apathetic as before.

"You are ill!" Tristrem exclaimed, advancing to him.

But Mr. Varick shook his head, and motioned him back. "It is nothing," he answered. "Let me see, you were saying——?"

"I am engaged to Miss Raritan."

"The daughter of——"

"Her father was Roanoke Raritan. He was minister somewhere—to England or to France, I believe."

While Tristrem was giving this information Mr. Varick went to the window. He looked at the occupant of the gilt cage, and ran a thumb through the wires. The bird ruffled its feathers, cocked its head, and edged gingerly along the perch, reproving the intrusive finger with the scorn and glitter of two eyes of bead. But the anger of the canary was brief. In a moment Mr. Varick left the cage, and turned again to his son.

"Nothing you could do," he said, "would please me better."

"Thank you," Tristrem answered, "I——"

"Are you to be married at once?"

"Not before November, sir."

"I wish it were sooner. I do not approve of protracted engagements. But, of course, you know your own business best. If I remember rightly, the father of this young lady did not leave much of a fortune, did he?"

"Nothing to speak of, I believe."

"You have my best wishes. The match is very suitable, very suitable. I wish you would say as much, with my compliments, to the young lady's mother. I would do so myself, but, as you know, I am something of an invalid. You might add that, too—and—er—I don't mean to advise you, but I would endeavor to hasten the ceremony. In such matters, it is usual for the young lady to be coy, but it is for the man to be pressing and resolute. I only regret that her father could not know of it. In regard to money, your allowance will have to be increased—well, I will attend to that. There is nothing else, is there? Oh, do me the favor not to omit to say that I am much pleased. I knew Miss Raritan's father." Mr. Varick looked up at the ceiling, and put his hand to his mouth. It was difficult to say whether he was concealing a smile or a yawn. "He would be pleased, I know." And with that Mr. Varick resumed his former position, and took up again the magazine.

"It is very good of you," Tristrem began; "I didn't know, of course—you see, I knew that if you saw the young lady—but what am I calling her a young lady for?" he asked, in an aside, of himself—"Miss Raritan, I mean," he continued aloud, "you would think me fortunate as a king's cousin." He paused. "I am sure," he reflected, "I don't know what I am talking about. What I say—is sheer imbecility. However," he continued, again, "I want to thank you. You have seen so little of me that I did not expect you would be particularly interested, I—I——"

He hesitated again, and then ceased speaking. He had been looking at his father, and something in his father's stare fascinated and disturbed his train of thought. For the moment he was puzzled. From his childhood he had felt that his father disliked him, though the reason of that dislike he had never understood. It was one of those things that you get so accustomed to that it is accepted, like baldness, as a matter of course, as a thing which had to be and could not be otherwise. To his grandfather, who was at once the most irascible and gentlest of men, and whom he had loved instinctively, from the first, with the unreasoning faith that children have—to him he had, in earlier days, spoken more than once of the singularity of his father's attitude. The old gentleman, however, had no explanation to give. Or, if he had one, he preferred to keep it to himself. But he petted the boy outrageously, with some idea of making up for it all, and of showing that he at least had love enough for two.

And now, as Tristrem gazed in his father's face, he seemed to decipher something that was not dislike—rather the contented look of one who learns of an enemy's disgrace, a compound of malice and of glee.

"That was all I had to say," Tristrem added, with his winning smile, as though apologizing for the lameness of the conclusion. And thereupon he left the room and went out to consult a jeweller and bear the tidings to other ears.

For some time he was absurdly happy. His grandfather received the announcement of the coming marriage with proper enthusiasm. He laughed sagaciously at Tristrem's glowing descriptions of the bride that was to be, and was for going to call on the mother and daughter at once, and was only prevented on learning that they had both left town.

"But I must write," he said, and write he did, two elaborate letters, couched in that phraseology at once recondite and simple which made our ancestors the delightful correspondents that they were. The letters were old-fashioned indeed. Some of the sentences were enlivened with the eccentricities of orthography which were in vogue in the days of the *Spectator*. The handwriting was infamous, and the signature on each was adorned with an enormous flourish. They were not models for a Perfect Letter Writer, but they were heartfelt and honest, and they served their purpose very well.

"And, Tristrem," the old gentleman said, when the addresses had been dried with a shower of sand and the letters despatched, "you must take her this, with my love. I gave it to your mother on her wedding day, and now it should go to her." From a little red case he took a diamond brooch, set in silver, which he polished reflectively on his sleeve. "She was very sweet, Tristrem, your mother was—a good girl, and a pretty one. Did I ever tell you about the time——"

And the old gentleman ran on with some anecdote of the dear dead days in which his heart was tombed. Tristrem listened with the interest of those that love. He had heard the story, and many others of a similar tenor, again and again, but, somehow, he never heard them too often. There was nothing wearisome to him in such chronicles; and as he sat listening, and now and then prompting with some forgotten detail, anyone who had happened on the scene would have accounted it pleasant to watch the young fellow and the old man talking together over the youth of her who had been mother to one and daughter to the other.

"See!" said Tristrem at last, when his grandfather had given the brooch into his keeping. "See! I have something for her too." And with that he displayed a ruby, unset, that was like a clot of blood. "I shall have it put in a ring," he explained, "but this might do for a bonnet-pin;" and then he produced a green stone, white-filmed, that had a heart of oscillating flame.

Mr. Van Norden had taken the ruby in his hand and held it off at arm's length, and then between two fingers, to the light, that he might the better judge of its beauty. But at the mention of the bonnet-pin he turned to look:

"Surely, Tristrem, you would not give her that; it's an opal."

"And what if it is?"

"But it is not lucky."

Tristrem smiled blithely, with the bravery that comes of nineteenth-century culture.

"It's a pearl with a soul," he answered, "that's what it is. And if Viola doesn't like it I'll send it to you."

"God forbid," Mr. Van Norden replied; "if anyone sent me an opal I would swear so hard that if the devil heard me he'd go in a corner and cross himself."

At this threat Tristrem burst out laughing, and the old gentleman, amused in spite of himself at the fantasy of his own speech, burst out laughing too.

Then there was more chat, and more reminiscences, and much planning as to how Tristrem should best assume the rank and appanages of the married state. Tristrem dined with his grandfather that evening, and when Mr. Van Norden started out to his club for a game of whist, Tristrem accompanied him as far as the club door.

When they parted, Tristrem was in such spirits that he could have run up to Central Park and back again. "Divinities of Pindar," he kept exclaiming—a phrase that he had caught somewhere—"divinities of Pindar, she is mine."

Thereafter, for several days, he lived, as all true lovers do, on air and the best tenderloins he could obtain.

VII.

One morning Tristrem found the sliced oranges companied by a note from Her. It was not long, but he read it so often that it became lengthy in spite of the writer. The cottage, it informed him, which had been taken for the summer, was becoming habitable. As yet but one of the hotels, and that the worst, was prepared for guests. In a fortnight, however, the others would begin to open their doors, and meanwhile if, in the course of the week, he care to run up, there was a room in the cottage at his disposal.

"In the course of the week," soliloquized Tristrem; "h'm—well, this afternoon is in the course of it, and this afternoon will I go."

Pleasured by the artfulness of his own sophistry, he procured a provision of *langues dorées*, a comestible of which she was fond, found at Tiffany's the ruby and opal set in accordance with orders already given, and at two o'clock boarded the Newport express.

The train reached New London before Tristrem had so much as glanced at a volume which he held in his hand. He had little need of anything to occupy his thoughts. His mind was a scenario in which he followed the changes and convolutions of an entertainment more alluring than any that romancer or playwright could convey. He was in that mood which we all of us have experienced, in which life seems not only worth living, but a fountain of delight as well. Were ever fields more green or sky more fair? And such a promise as the future held! In his hearing was a choir of thrushes, and on his spirit had been thrown a mantle so subtle, yet of texture so insistent, that no thought not wholly pure could pierce the woof or find a vantage-ground therein. He was in that mood in which one feels an ascension of virtues, the companionship of unviolated illusions, the pomp and purple of worship, a communion with all that is best, a repulsion of all that is base—that mood in which hymns mount unsummoned from the heart.

He was far away, but the Ideal was at his side. The past was a mirror, mirroring nothing save his own preparation and the dream of the coming of her. And now she had come, fairer than the fairest vision and desire that ever visited a poet starving in a garret. To be worthy of her, even in the slightest measure, what was there that he would leave undone? And as the train brought him to his journey's end, he repeated to himself, gravely and decorously, and with the earnestness and sincerity of the untried, the grave covenants of the marriage pact.

On descending at the station he remembered, for the first time, that he had omitted to send Miss Raritan an avant-courier in the shape of a telegram. It is one of the oddities of hazard that, in turning down one street instead of turning up another, a man's existence, and not his own alone, but that of others also, may seem to be wholly changed thereby. The term *seem* is used advisedly, for, with a better understanding of the interconnection of cause and effect, chance has been outlawed by science, and in the operations of consistent laws the axiom, "Whatever will be, Is," has passed to the kindergarten. Tristrem thought of this months afterward. He remembered then, that that morning he had started out with the intention of sending a telegram from the club, but on the way there he had thought of the chocolate which Viola preferred, and, after turning into Broadway to purchase it, he had drifted into Tiffany's, and from there he had returned to Waverley Place, the message unsent and forgotten. He recalled these incidents months later, but for the moment he merely felt a vague annoyance at his own neglect.

There was a negro at the station, the driver of a coach in whose care Tristrem placed himself, and presently the coach rattled over a road that skirted the sea, and drew up at the gate of a tiny villa. On the porch Mrs. Raritan was seated, and when she recognized her visitor she came down the path, exclaiming her pleasure and welcome. It was evident at once that she had been gratified by her daughter's choice.

"But we didn't expect you," she said. "Viola told me you would not come before Saturday. I am glad you did, though; as yet there's hardly a soul in the place. Viola has gone riding. It's after seven, isn't it? She ought to be back now. Why didn't you send us word? We would have met you at the train."

They had found seats on the porch. Tristrem explained his haste, apologizing for the neglect to wire. The haste seemed pardonable to Mrs. Raritan, and the attendant absent-mindedness easily understood. And so for some moments they talked together. Tristrem delivered his father's message, and learned that Mr. Van Norden's letters had been received. Some word was even said of the possibility of a September wedding. And then a little plot was concocted. Dinner would be served almost immediately, so soon, in fact, as Viola returned. Meanwhile, Tristrem would go to his room, Mrs. Raritan would say nothing of his arrival, but, when dinner was announced, a servant would come to his door, and then he was to appear and give Viola the treat and pleasure of a genuine surprise.

This plan was acted on at once. Tristrem was shown to the room which he was to occupy, and proceeded to get his things in order. From his shirt-box, which, with his valise, had already been brought upstairs, he took the ring, the brooch, the pin, and placed them on the mantel. Then he found other garments, and began to dress. In five minutes he was in readiness, but as yet he heard nothing indicative of Viola's return. He went to the window and looked out. Above the trees, in an adjacent property, there loomed a tower. The window was at the back of the house; he could not see the ocean, but he heard its resilient sibilants, and from the garden came the hum of insects. It had grown quite dark, but still there was no sign of Viola's return.

He took up the volume which he had brought with him in the cars. It was the *Rime Nuove* of Carducci, and with the fancies of that concettist of modern Rome he stayed his impatience for a while. There was one octave that had appealed to him before. He read it twice, and was about to endeavor to repeat the lines from memory, when through the open window he heard the clatter of horses' hoofs, the roll of wheels; it was evident that some conveyance had stopped at the gate of the villa. Then came the sound of hurrying feet, a murmur of voices, and abruptly the night was cut with the anguish of a woman's cry.

Tristrem rushed from the room and down the stairs. Through the open door beyond a trembling star was visible, and in the road a group of undistinguished forms.

"She's only fainted," someone was saying; "she was right enough a minute ago."

Before the sentence was completed, Tristrem was at the gate. Hatless, with one hand ungloved and the other clutching a broken whip, the habit rent from hem to girdle, dust-covered and dishevelled, the eyes closed, and in the face the pallor and contraction of mortal pain, Viola Raritan lay, waist-supported, in her mother's arms.

"Help me with her to the house," the mother moaned. Then noticing Tristrem at her side, "She's been thrown," she added; "I knew she would be—I knew it——"

And as Tristrem reached to aid her with the burden, the girl's eyes opened, "It's nothing." She raised her ungloved hand, "I—" and swooned again.

They bore her into a little sitting-room, and laid her down. Mrs. Raritan followed, distraught with fright. In her helplessness, words came from her unsequenced and obscure. But soon she seemed to feel the need of action. One servant she despatched for a physician, from another a restorative was obtained. And Tristrem, meanwhile, knelt at the girl's side, beating her hand with his. It had been scratched, he noticed, as by a briar, and under the nails were stains such as might come from plucking berries that are red.

As he tried to take from her the whip, that he might rub the hand that held it too, the girl recovered consciousness again. The swoon had lasted but a moment or so, yet to him who watched it had been unmeasured time. She drew away the hand he held, and raising herself she looked at him; to her lips there came a tremulousness and her eyes filled.

"My darling," Mrs. Raritan sobbed, "are you hurt? Tell me. How did it happen? Did the horse run away with you. Oh, Viola, I knew there would be an accident. Where are you hurt? Did the horse drag you?"

The girl turned to her mother almost wonderingly. It seemed to Tristrem that she was not yet wholly herself.

"Yes," she answered; "no, I mean—no, he didn't, it was an accident, he shied. *Do* get me upstairs." And with that her head fell again on the cushion.

Tristrem sought to raise her, but she motioned him back and caught her mother's hand, and rising with its assistance she let the arm circle her waist, and thus supported she suffered herself to be led away.

Tristrem followed them to the hall. On the porch a man loitered, hat in hand; as Tristrem approached he rubbed the brim reflectively.

"I saw the horse as good as an hour ago," he said, "I was going to Caswell's." And with this information he crooked his arm and made a backward gesture. "It's down yonder on the way to the Point," he explained. "As I passed Hazard's I looked in the cross-road—I call it a road, but after you get on a bit it's nothing more than a cow-path, all bushes and suchlike. But just up the road I see'd the horse. He was nibbling grass as quiet as you please. I didn't pay no attention, I thought he was tied. Well, when I was coming back I looked again; he wasn't there, but just as I got to the turn I heard somebody holloaing, and I stopped. A man ran up and says to me, 'There's a lady hurt herself, can't you give her a lift?' 'Where?' says I. 'Down there,' he says, 'back of Hazard's; she's been thrown.' So I turned round, and sure enough there she was, by the fence, sort of dazed like. I says, 'Are you hurt, miss?' and she says, 'No,' but could I bring her here, and then I see'd that her dress was torn. She got in, and I asked her where her hat was, and she said it was back there, but it didn't make no difference, she wanted to get home. And when we were driving on here I told her as how I see'd the horse, and I asked if it wasn't one of White's, and she said, 'Yes, it was,' and I was a-going to ask where she was thrown, but she seemed sort of faint, and, sure enough, just as we got here away she went. I always says women-folk ought not to be let on horseback, she might have broke her neck; like as not——"

"You have been very kind," Tristrem answered, "very kind, indeed."

During the entire scene he had not said a word. The spectacle of Viola fainting on the roadside, the fear that she might be maimed, the trouble at her pallor—these things had tied his tongue; and even now, as he spoke, his voice was not assured, and a hand with which he fumbled in his waistcoat trembled so that the roll of bills which he drew out fell on the porch at his feet. He stooped and picked it up.

"If Mrs. Raritan were here, she would thank you as I do," he continued. "I wish—" and he was about to make some present, but the man drew back.

"That's all right, I don't want no pay for that."

"I beg your pardon," Tristrem answered, "I know you do not. Tell me, are you married?"

The man laughed.

"Yes, I am, and I got the biggest boy you ever see. He's going on four years and he weighs a ton."

"I wish you would do me a favor. Let me make him a little present."

But even to this the man would not listen. He was reluctant to accept so much as thanks. Having done what good he could, he was anxious to go his way—the sort of man that one has to visit the seashore to find, and who, when found, is as refreshing as the breeze.

As he left the porch, he looked back. "Here's the doctor," he said, and passed on into the night.

While the physician visited the patient, Tristrem paced the sitting-room counting the minutes till he could have speech with him, himself. And when at last he heard the stairs creak, he was out in the hall, prepared to question and intercept. The physician was most reassuring. There was nothing at all the matter. By morning Miss Raritan would be up and about. She had had a shock, no doubt. She was upset, and a trifle nervous, but all she needed was a good night's rest, with a chop and a glass of claret to help her to it. If sleep were elusive, then a bromide. But that was all. If she had been seventy a tumble like that might have done for her, but at nineteen! And the doctor left the house, reflecting that were not educated people the most timorous of all, the emoluments of his profession would be slight.

Whether or not Miss Raritan found the chop and claret sufficient, or whether she partook of a bromide as well, is not a part of history. In a little while after the physician's departure a servant brought word to Tristrem that for the moment Mrs. Raritan was unable to leave her daughter, but if he would have his dinner then, Mrs. Raritan would see him later. Such was the revulsion of feeling that Tristrem, to whom, ten minutes before, the mere mention of food would have been distasteful, sat down, and ate like a wolf. The meal finished, he went out on the porch. There was no moon as yet, but the sky was brilliant with the lights of other worlds. Before him was the infinite, in the air was the scent of sea-weed, and beyond, the waves leaped up and fawned upon the bluffs. And as he stood and watched it all, the servant came to him with Mrs. Raritan's apologies. She thought it better, the maid explained, not to leave Miss Raritan just yet, and would Mr. Varick be good enough to excuse her for that evening?

"Wait a second," he answered, and went to his room. He found the jewels, and brought them down-stairs. "Take these to Miss Raritan," he said, and on a card he wrote some word of love, which he gave with the trinkets to the maid. "*La parlate d'amor*," he murmured, as the servant left to do his bidding, and then he went again to his room, and sat down at the window companioned only by the stars. From beyond, the boom and retreating wash of waves was still audible, and below in the garden he caught, now and then, the spark and glitter of a firefly gyrating in loops of gold, but the tower which he had noticed on arriving was lost in the night.

It was in that direction, he told himself, that the accident must have occurred. And what was it, after all? As yet he had not fully understood. Had the horse stumbled, or had he bolted and thrown her? If he had only been there! And as his fancy evoked the possibilities of that ride, he saw a terrified brute tearing along a deserted road, carrying the exquisite girl straight to some sudden death, and, just when the end was imminent, his own muscles hardened into steel, he had him by the bit and, though dragged by the impetus, at last he held him, and she was safe. She was in his arms, her own about his neck, and were he a knight-errant and she some gracious princess, what sweeter guerdon could he claim?

But one thing preoccupied him. In the vertiginous flight she had lost something—her whip, no, her hat—and it was incumbent on him to restore it to her. Very softly, then, that he might not disturb her, he opened the door. The house was hushed, and in a moment he was on the road. He could see the tower now; it was illuminated, and it seemed to him odd that he had not noticed the illumination before. It was that way, he knew, back of Hazard's, and he hurried along in the direction which the man had indicated. The insects had stilled their murmur, and the sky was more obscure, but the road was clear.

He hurried on, and as he hurried he heard steps behind him, hurrying too. He turned his head; behind him was a woman running, and who, as she ran, cast a shadow that was monstrous. In the glimpse that he caught of her he saw that she was bare of foot and that her breast was uncovered. Her skirt was tattered and her hair was loose. He turned again, the face was hideous. The eyes squinted, lustreless and opaque, the nose was squat, the chin retreated, the forehead was seamed with scars, and the mouth, that stretched to the ears, was extended with laughter. As she ran she took her teeth out one by one, replacing them with either hand. And still she laughed, a silent laughter, her thin lips distorted as though she mocked the world.

Tristrem, overcome by the horror of that laughter, felt as agonized as a child pursued. There was a fence at hand, a vacant lot, and across it a light glimmered. Away he sped. In the field his foot caught in a bramble; he fell, and could not rise, but he heard her coming and, with a great effort just as she was on him, he was up again, distancing her with ever-increasing space. The light was just beyond. He saw now it came from the tower; there was another fence, he was over it; the door was barred; no, it opened; he was safe!

In the middle of the room, circular as befits a tower, was a cradle, and in the cradle was a little boy. As Tristrem looked at him he smiled; it was, he knew, the child of the man to whom he had spoken that evening. One hand was under the pillow, but the other, that lay on the coverlid, held Viola's hat. He bent over to examine it; the fingers that held it were grimy and large, and, as he looked closer, he saw that it was not a child, but the man himself. Before he had an opportunity to account for the delusion he heard the gallop of feet and a thunder at the door. It was she! He wheeled like a rat surprised. There was a lateral exit, through which he fled, and presently he found himself in a corridor that seemed endless in extension. The man evidently had left the cradle and preceded him, for Tristrem saw him putting on a great-coat some distance ahead. In his feverish fright he thought, could he but disguise himself with that, he might pass out unobserved, and he ran on to supplicate for an exchange of costume; but when he reached the place where the man had stood he had gone, vanished through a dead wall, and down the corridor he heard her come. He could hear her bare feet patter on the stones. Oh, God, what did she wish of him? And no escape, not one. He was in her power, immured with her forevermore. He called for help, and beat at the walls, and ever nearer she came, swifter than disease, and more appalling than death. His nails sank in his flesh, he raised a hand to stay the beating of his heart, and then at once she was upon him, felling him to the ground as a ruffian fells his mistress, her knees were on his arms, he was powerless, dumb with dread, and in his face was the fetor of her breath. Her eyes were no longer lustreless, they glittered like twin stars, and still she laughed, her naked breast heaving with the convulsions of her mirth. "I am Truth," she bawled, and laughed again. And with that Tristrem awoke, suffocating, quivering, and outwearied as though he had run a race and lost it.

He sat awhile, broken by the horror of the dream. The palms of his hands were not yet dry. But soon he bestirred himself, and went to the door; the lights had been extinguished; he closed it again, and, with the aid of some candles, he prepared for bed. He would have read a little, but he was fatigued, tired by the emotions of the day, and when at last he lay down it was an effort to rise again and put out the candle. How long he lay in darkness, a second, an hour, he could not afterward recall; it seemed to him that he had drowsed off at once, but suddenly he started, trembling from head to foot. He had heard Viola's voice soaring to its uttermost tension. "Coward," she had called. And then all was still. He listened, he even went to the door, but the house was wrapped in silence.

"Bah!" he muttered, "I am entertaining a procession of nightmares." And in a few moments he was again asleep.

VIII.

At dawn he awoke refreshed. The sun rose from the ocean like an indolent girl from a bath. Before the house was astir he was out of doors exploring the land. He strolled past the row of hotels that front the sea, and pausing a moment at the Casino, fragrant then, and free of the stench of drink that is the outcome of the later season, he wondered how it was that, given money, and possibly brains, it was necessary to make a building as awkward as was that. And then he strayed to the shore, past the tenantless bath-houses, and on through the glories of the morning to the untrodden beach beyond.

As he walked, the village faded in the haze. The tide was low and the sand firm and hard. The waves broke leisurely in films and fringes of white, gurgling an invitation to their roomy embrace. And when the hotels were lost in the distance and the solitude was murmurous with nature alone, Tristrem, captivated by the allurements of the sea, went down into the waves and clasped them to him as lovers clasp those they love.

The sun was well on its amble to the zenith before he returned to the cottage. His hostess, he found, had not yet appeared, and as breakfast seemed to be served in that pleasant fashion which necessitates nothing, not even an appetite, Tristrem drank his coffee in solitude. And as he idled over the meal he recalled the horrors of the night, and smiled. The air of the morning, the long and quiet stroll, the plunge in the sea, and the after-bath of sunlight that he had taken stretched full length on the sand, had dissipated the enervating emotions of dream and brought him in their stead a new invigoration. He was about to begin the dithyrambs of the day before, when the servant appeared, bearing a yellow envelope, and a book in which he was to put his name. He gave the receipt and opened the message, wonderingly.

"*Please come to town,*" it ran, "*your father is dying.—Robert Harris.*"

"Your father is dying," he repeated. "H'm. Robert Harris. I never knew before what the butler's first name was. But what has that to do with it? There are times when I am utterly imbecile. Your father is dying. Yes, of course, I must go at once. But it isn't possible. H'm. I remember. He looked ghastly when I saw him. I suppose—I ought to—good God, why should I attempt to feign a sorrow that I do not feel? It is his own fault. I would have—But there, what is the use?"

He bit his nail; he was perplexed at his absence of sensibility. "And yet," he mused, "in his way he has been kind to me. He has been kind; that is, if it be kindness in a father to let a son absolutely alone. After all, filial affection must be like patriotism, ingrained as an obligation, a thing to blush at if not possessed. Yet then, again, if a country acts like a step-mother to its children, if a father treats a son as a guardian might treat a ward, the ties are conventional; and on what shall affection subsist? It was he who called me into being, and, having done so, he assumed duties which he should not have shirked. It was not for him to make himself a stranger to me; it was for him to teach me to honor him so much, to love him so well that at his death my head would be bowed in prostrations of grief. I used to try to school myself to think that it was only his way; that, outwardly cold and undemonstrative, his heart was warm as another's. But—well, it may have been, it may have been. After all, if I can't grieve, I would cross the continent to spare him a moment's pain. It was he, I suppose, who told Harris to wire. Yes, I must hurry."

He called the servant to him. "Can you tell me, please, when the next train goes?" But the servant had no knowledge whereon to base a reply. She suggested, however, that information might be obtained at an inn which stood a short distance up the road. He scribbled a few lines on a card, and gave it to the woman. "Take that to Miss Raritan, please, will you?" he said, and left the house.

At the inn a very large individual sat on the stoop, coatless, a straw covering of a remoter summer far back on his head, and his feet turned in. He listened to Tristrem with surly indifference, and spat profusely. He didn't know; he reckoned the morning train had gone.

"Hay, Alf," he called out to the negro who had taken Tristrem from the station the night before, and who was then driving by, "when's the next train go?"

"'Bout ten minutes; I just took a party from Taylor's."

"Thank you," said Tristrem to the innkeeper, who spat again by way of acknowledgment. "Can you take me to the station?" he asked the negro; and on receiving an affirmative reply, he told him to stop at Mrs. Raritan's for his traps.

As Tristrem entered the gate he saw Viola's assistant of the preceding evening drive up, waving a hat.

"I got it," the man cried out, "here it is. First time it ever passed a night out of doors, I'll bet. And none the worse for it, either." He handed it over to Tristrem. "I dreamt about you last night," he added.

"That's odd," Tristrem answered, "I dreamed about you." The man laughed at this as had he never heard anything so droll. "Well, I swan!" he exclaimed, and cracked his whip with delight. His horse started. "Here," he said, "I near forgot. Whoa, there, can't you. This goes with the hat." And he crumpled a handkerchief in his hand, and tossing it to Tristrem, he let the horse continue his way unchecked.

The hat which the man had found did not indeed look as though it had passed a night on the roadside. Save for an incidental speck or two it might have come fresh from a bandbox. Tristrem carried it into the cottage, and was placing it on the hall-table when Mrs. Raritan appeared.

"I am so sorry," she began, "Viola has told me———"

"How is she? May I not see her?"

"She scarcely slept last night."

Tristrem looked in the lady's face. The lids of her eyes were red and swollen.

"But may I not see her? May I not, merely for a moment."

"She is sleeping now," Mrs. Raritan answered; "perhaps," she added, "it is better that you should not. The doctor has been here. He says that she should be quiet. But you will come back, will you not? Truly I sympathize with you."

Mrs. Raritan's eyes filled with tears, but to what they were due, who shall say? She seemed to Tristrem unaccountably nervous and distressed.

"There is nothing serious the matter, is there?" he asked, anxiously. And at the question, Mrs. Raritan almost choked. She shook her head, however, but Tristrem was not assured. "I *must* see her," he said, and he made as would he mount the stair.

"Mr. Varick! she is asleep. She has had a wretched night. When you are able to come back, it will be different. But if you care for her, let her be."

The protest was almost incoherent. Mrs. Raritan appeared beside herself with anxiety.

"Forgive me," said Tristrem, "I did not mean to vex you. Nor would I disturb her." He paused a second, dumbly and vaguely afflicted. "You will tell her, will you not?" he added; "tell her this, that I wanted to see her. Mrs. Raritan, my whole life is wrapped up in her." He hesitated again. "You are tired too, I can see. You were up with her last night, were you not?"

Mrs. Raritan bowed her head.

"You must forgive me," he repeated, "I did not understand. Tell me," he continued, "last night I awoke thinking that I heard her calling. Did she call?"

"Call what?"

"I thought—you see I was half, perhaps wholly asleep, but I thought I heard her voice. I was mistaken, was I not?"

"Yes, you must have been."

The negro had brought down the luggage, and stood waiting at the gate.

"You will tell her—Mrs. Raritan—I love her with all my heart and soul."

The lady's lips quivered. "She knows it, and so do I."

"You will ask her to write."

"Yes, I will do so."

Tristrem took her hand in his. "Tell her from me," he began, but words failed him, it was his face that completed the message. In a moment more he was in the coach on his way to the station.

There was a brisk drive along the sea, a curve was rounded, and the station stood in sight. And just as the turn was made Tristrem caught the shriek of a whistle.

"There she goes," the negro exclaimed, "you ought to have been spryer."

"Has the train gone?" Tristrem asked.

"Can't you see her? I knew you'd be late." The man was insolent in his familiarity, but Tristrem did not seem to notice it.

"I would have given much not to be," he said.

At this the negro became a trifle less uncivil. "Would you ree-ly like to catch that train?" he asked.

"I would indeed."

"Is it worth twenty-five dollars to you?"

Tristrem nodded.

"Well, boss, I tell you. That train stops at Peacedale, and at Wakefield she shunts off till the mail passes. Like as not the express is late. If I get you to Kingston before the Newport passes, will you give me twenty-five?"

"If I make the connection I will give you fifty."

"That's talking. You'll get there, boss. Just lay back and count your thumbs."

The negro snapped his whip, and soon Tristrem was jolted over one of the worst and fairest roads of New England, through a country for which nature has done her best, and where only the legislator is vile. One hamlet after another was passed, and still the coach rolled on.

"We'll get there," the negro repeated from time to time, and to encourage his fare he lashed the horses to their utmost speed. Peacedale was in the distance;

Wakefield was passed, and in a cloud of dust they tore through Kingston and reached the station just as the express steamed up.

"I told you I'd do it," the negro exclaimed, exultingly. "I'll get checks for your trunks."

A minute or two more, and the checks were obtained; the negro was counting a roll of bills, and in a drawing-room car Tristrem was being whirled to New York.

For several hours he sat looking out at the retreating uplands, villages, and valleys. But after a while he remembered the scantiness of his breakfast, and, summoning the porter, he obtained from him some food and drink. By this time the train had reached New Haven, and there Tristrem alighted to smoke a cigarette. He was, however, unable to finish it before the whistle warned him that he should be aboard again. The porter, who had been gratified by a tip, then told him that there was a smoking compartment in the car beyond the one in which he had sat, and, as the train moved on, Tristrem went forward in the direction indicated.

The compartment was small, with seats for two on one side, and for three, or for four at most, on the other. As Tristrem entered it he saw that the larger sofa was occupied by one man, who lay out on it, full length, his face turned to the partition. Tristrem took a seat opposite him, and lit a fresh cigarette. As he smoked he looked at the reclining form of his *vis-à-vis*. About the man's neck a silk handkerchief had been rolled, but one end had come undone and hung loosely on the cushion, and as Tristrem looked he noticed that on the neck was a wound, unhealed and fresh, a line of excoriation, that neither steel nor shot could have caused, but which might have come from a scratch. But, after all, what business was it of his? And he turned his attention again to the retreating uplands and to the villages that starred the route.

When the cigarette was done, he stood up to leave the compartment. But however quietly he had moved, he seemed to arouse his neighbor, who turned heavily, as though to change his position. As he did so, Tristrem saw that it was Royal Weldon, and that on his face was a bruise. He would have spoken, for Weldon was looking at him, but he recalled the wanton lie of the week before, and as he hesitated whether to speak or pass on, Weldon half rose. "Damn you," he said, "you are everywhere." Then he lay down, turning his face again to the wall, and Tristrem, without a word, went to the other car and found his former seat.

Two hours later he reached his home. He let himself in with a latch-key, and rang the bell. But when Harris appeared he knew at once, by the expression which the butler assumed, that he had come too late.

"When did it happen?" he asked.

"It was last evening, sir; he came in from his drive and inquired for you, sir. I said that you had gone out of town, and showed him the address you left. When I went to hannounce dinner, sir, he was sitting in his arm-chair with his hat on. I thought he was asleep. I sent for Dr. McMasters, sir, but it was no use. Dr. McMasters said it was the 'art, sir."

"You have notified my grandfather, have you not?"

"Yes, sir, I did, sir; Mr. Van Norden came in this morning, and left word as how he would like to see you when you got back, sir."

"Very good. Call Davis, and get my things from the cabman."

"Yes, sir; thank you, sir. I beg pardon, sir," he added, "would you wish some dinner? There's a nice fillet and a savory."

IX.

The morning after the funeral Tristrem received a letter from Mrs. Raritan, and a little later a small package by express. The letter was not long, and its transcription is unnecessary. It was to the effect that on maturer consideration Viola had decided that the engagement into which she had entered was untenable. To this decision Mrs. Raritan felt herself reluctantly obliged to concur. It was not that Mr. Varick was one whom she would be unwilling to welcome as her daughter's husband. On the contrary, he was in many respects precisely what she most desired. But Viola was young; she felt that she had a vocation to which marriage would be an obstacle, and in the circumstances Viola was the better judge. In any event, Mr. Varick was requested to consider the decision as irrevocable. Then followed a few words of sympathy and a line of condolence expressive of Mrs. Raritan's regret that the breaking of the engagement should occur at a time when Tristrem was in grievous affliction.

In the package were the jewels.

Tristrem read the letter as though he were reading some accusation of felony levelled at him in the public press. If it had been a meteor which had fallen at his feet he could not have wondered more. Indeed, it was surprise that he felt. It was not anger or indignation; they were after-comers. For the moment he was merely bewildered. It seemed to him incredible that such a thing could be. He read the letter again, and even examined the post-mark. At first he was for starting at once for Narragansett. If he could but see Viola! The excuse about a vocation was nonsense. Had he not told her that if she insisted on going on the stage, he would sit in the stalls and applaud. No, it was not that; it was because—After all, it was his own fault; if he had been unable to make himself beloved, why should the engagement continue? But had an opportunity been given him? He had not had speech with her since that evening when she had drawn his face to hers. No, it could not be that.

He bowed his head, and then Anger came and sat at his side. What had he done to Destiny that he should be to it the play-thing that he was? But she; she was more voracious even than Fate. No, it was damnable. Why should she take his heart and torment it? Why, having given love, should she take it away? He was contented enough until he saw her. Why had she come to him as the one woman in the world, luring him on; yes, for she had lured him on? Why had she made him love her as he could never love again, and just when she placed her hand in his,—a mist, a phantom, a reproach? Why had she done so? Why was the engagement untenable? Untenable, indeed, why was it untenable? Why—why—why? And in the increasing exasperation of the moment, Tristrem did a thing that, with him, was unusual. He rang the bell, and bade the servant bring him drink.

It was on the afternoon of that day that he learned the tenor of his father's will. It affected him as a chill affects a man smitten with fever. He accepted it as a matter of course. It was not even the last drop; the cup was full as it stood. What was it to him that he had missed being one of the richest men in New York in comparison to the knowledge that even had he the mines of Ormuz and of Ind, the revenue would be as useless to him as the hands of the dead? Was she to be bought? Had she not taken herself away before the contents of the will were reported? He might be able to call the world his own, and it would avail him nothing.

The will left him strangely insensible, though, after all, one may wonder whether winter is severer than autumn to a flower once dead.

But if the will affected Tristrem but little, it stirred Dirck Van Norden to paroxysms of wrath. "He ought to have his ghost kicked," he said, in confidential allusion to Erastus Varick. "It's a thing that cries out to heaven. And don't you tell me, sir, that nothing can be done."

The lawyer with whom he happened to be in consultation said there were many things that could be done. Indeed, he was reassuringly fecund in resources. In the first place, the will was holographic. That, of course, mattered nothing; it only pointed a moral. Laymen should not draw up their own wills. For that matter, even professionals should be as wary of so doing as physicians are of doctoring themselves. And the lawyer instanced legal luminaries, judges whose *obiter dicta* and opinions *in banco* were cited and received with the greatest respect, and yet through whose wills, drawn up, mark you, by their own skilled hands, coaches and tandems had been driven full speed. In regard to the will of the deceased there was this to be said, it would not hold water. Chapter 360, Laws of 1860, declares that no person having a husband, wife, child, or parent, shall by his or her last will and testament, devise or bequeath to any benevolent, charitable, scientific, literary, religious, or missionary society, association, or corporation, in trust or otherwise, more than one-half part of his or her estate.

"But he devised the whole."

"Yes, so he did; but in devising it he overlooked that very wise law. My opinion in the matter is this. When, may I ask, was your grandson born?"

"He was born on the 10th of June, 1859."

"Exactly. The late Mr. Varick determined, on the birth of your grandson, that the property should go over. His reasons for so determining are immaterial. Rufus K. Taintor, the ablest man, sir, that ever sat on the bench or addressed it, drew up the will at that time in accordance with instructions received. Some years later, Taintor died of apoplexy, and he died, too, as you doubtless remember, after the delivery of that famous speech in the Besalul divorce case. Well, sir, what I make of the matter is this. The late Mr. Varick, relying on Taintor's ability, and possessing possibly some smattering of law of his own, recopied the will every time the fancy took him to make minor alterations in the general distribution of the trust. Consequently his last will and testament, having been made since the passage of the law of 1860, is nugatory and void as to one-half the bequest, and your grandson may still come in for a very pretty sum."

"He ought to have it all," said Mr. Van Norden, decidedly.

"I don't dispute that, sir, in the least—and my opinion is that he will get it. This will is dated five days previous to Mr. Varick's demise. Now, according to the law of 1848, Chapter 319, and, if I remember rightly, Section 6, no such bequest as the deceased's is valid in any will which shall not have been made and executed at least two months before the death of the testator. That, sir, I consider an extremely wise bit of legislation. The law of 1860, which I quoted, vitiates the will as to one-half the bequest; the law of 1848 does away with the will altogether. Practically speaking, your son-in-law might just as well have died intestate. Though, between ourselves, if Mr. Varick had not been ignorant of these laws, and had not, in consequence of his ignorance, made a disposition of certain private documents the contents of which are easily guessed, your grandson would have merely a *prima facie* right to have the will set aside; for, if you remember, these laws were passed only to provide for the possible interests of a surviving husband, wife, or *child*."

He emphasized the last word, and, as his meaning grew clear to Mr. Van Norden, that gentleman got very red in the face. He rang the bell.

"Thank you, sir," he said. "I shall be indebted if you will send me your account. And I shall be particularly indebted if you will send it at your very earliest convenience. Henry, get this—this—get this gentleman his hat and see him to the street."

Unfortunately for those that practise, there are a great many more lawyers in New York than one. And before the last will and testament of Erastus Varick came up for probate, Mr. Van Norden experienced slight difficulty in retaining another attorney to defend Tristrem's interests. The matter, of course, was set down for a hearing, and came up on the calendar three months later.

Of the result of that hearing the reader has been already informed, and then it was that Tristrem was taxed with old-world folly.

X.

In years gone by it had been Mr. Van Norden's custom to pass the heated term at Rockaway. But when Rockaway became a popular resort, Mr. Van Norden, like the sensible man that he was, discovered that his own house was more comfortable than a crowded hotel. This particular summer, therefore, he passed as usual in New York, and Tristrem, who had moved to his house, kept him company. June was not altogether disagreeable, but in July the city was visited by a heat at once insistent and enervating. In August it was cooler, as our Augusts are apt to be; yet the air was lifeless, and New York was not a nosegay. During these months Tristrem was as lifeless as the air. In his first need of sympathy he had gone to the irascible and kind-hearted old gentleman and told him of the breaking of the engagement, and, he might have added, of his heart, though in the telling he sought, with a lover's fealty, to palliate the grievousness of the cruelty to which he had been subjected.

"It is this way," he said; "Viola, I think, feels that she does not know me sufficiently well. After all, we have seen but little of each other, and if she accepted me, it was on the spur of the moment. Since then she has thought of it more seriously. It is for me to win her, not for her to throw herself in my arms. That is what she has thought. She may seem capricious; and what if she does? Your knowledge of women has, I am sure, made you indulgent."

"Not in the least," Mr. Van Norden answered. And then, for the time being, the subject was dropped.

It was this semi-consolatory view which Tristrem took of the matter after the effect of the first shock had lost its force. But when he received the bundle of letters, together with the Panama hat, which, through some splendid irony, had been devised to him in the only clause of the will in which his name was mentioned, it was as though a flash had rent the darkness and revealed in one quick glare an answer to the enigma in which he groped.

The letters were few in number—a dozen at most—and they were tied together with a bit of faded ribbon. They were all in the same hand, one and all contained protestations of passionate love, and each was signed in full, Roanoke Raritan. The envelope which held them was addressed to Mrs. Erastus Varick.

It was then that he saw the reason of his disinheritance, and it was then that he understood the cause of Viola's withdrawal. It was evident to him that Mrs. Raritan possessed either thorough knowledge of the facts, or else that she had some inkling of them which her feminine instinct had supplemented into evidence, and which had compelled her to forbid the banns. There were, however, certain things which he could not make clear to his mind. Why had Mrs. Raritan treated him with such consideration? She had known from the first that he loved her daughter. And after the engagement, if she wished it broken, why had she allowed Viola to invite him to the Pier?

These things were at first inexplicable to him. Afterward he fancied that it might be that Mrs. Raritan, originally uninformed, had become so only through the man whom he had believed was his father, after the announcement of the engagement had been made to him, and possibly through some communication which had only reached her after his sudden death. This explanation he was inclined to accept, and he was particularly inclined to do so on recalling the spasm which had agitated the deceased when he had come to him with the intelligence of the engagement, and the nervous excitement which Mrs. Raritan displayed on the morning when he left for town.

This explanation he accepted later—but in the horror of the situation in which he first found himself his mind declined to act. He had never known his mother, but her fame he had cherished as one cherishes that which is best and most perfect of all. And abruptly that fame was tarnished, as some fair picture might be sullied by a splash and splatter of mud. And as though that were insufficient, the letters which devastated his mother's honor brought him a hideous suspicion, and one which developed into certainty, that his father and the father of the girl whom he loved were one and the same.

It is not surprising, then, that during the summer months Tristrem was as lifeless as the air he breathed. His grandfather noticed the change—he would have been blind indeed had he not—and he urged him to leave New York. But at each remonstrance Tristrem shook his head with persistent apathy. What did it matter to him where he was? If New York, instead of being merely hot and uncomfortable, had been cholera-smitten, and the prey of pest, Tristrem's demeanor would not have altered. There are people whom calamity affects like a tonic, who rise from misfortune refreshed; there are others on whom disaster acts like a soporific, and he was one of the latter. For three months he did not open a book, the daily papers were taken from him unread, and if during that time he had lost his reason, it is probable that his insanity would have consisted in sitting always with eyes fixed, without laughing, weeping, or changing place.

But after the hearing in the Surrogate's Court there was a change of scene. The will was set aside, and the estate, of which Tristrem had taken absolutely no thought whatever, reverted to him. It was then that he made it over in its entirety to the institution to which it had been originally devised; and it was in connection with the disposal of the property, a disposal which he effected as a matter of course, and as the only right and proper thing for him to do, that he enjoyed a memorable interview with his grandfather.

He had not spoken to Mr. Van Norden about the letters, and the old gentleman, through some restraining sense of delicacy, had hesitated to question. Besides, he was confident that the estate would be Tristrem's, and thus assured, it seemed unnecessary to him to touch on a matter to which Tristrem had not alluded, and which was presumably distasteful to him. But when he learned what Tristrem had done, he looked upon the matter in a different light, and attacked him very aggressively the next day.

"I can understand perfectly," he said, "that you should decline to hold property on what you seem to regard as a legal quibble. But I should be very much gratified to learn in what your judgment is superior to that of the Legislature, and why you should refuse that to which you had as clear and indefeasible a claim as I have to this fob on my waistcoat. I should be really very much gratified to learn——"

Tristrem looked at his grandfather very much as though he had been asked to open a wound. But he answered nothing. He got the letters and placed them in the old gentleman's hand.

Mr. Van Norden glanced at one, and then turned to Tristrem. It was evident that he was in the currents of conflicting and retroacting emotions. He made as though he would speak, yet for the time being the intensity of his feelings prevented him. He took up the letters again and eyed them, shaking his head as he did so with the anger of one enraged at the irreparable, and conscious of the futility of the wrath.

In the lives of most men and women there are moments in which they are pregnant with words. The necessity of speech is so great that until the parturition is accomplished they experience the throes of suffocation. If no listener be at hand, there are at least the walls. Mr. Van Norden was standing near to Tristrem, but that he might be the better assured of his attention, he caught him by the arm, and addressed him in abrupt, disjointed sentences, in a torrent of phrases, unconnected, as though others than himself beat their vocables from his mouth. His words were so tumultuous that they assailed the gates of speech, as spectators at the sight of flame crowd the exits of a hall, and issue, some as were they hurled from catapults, others, maimed, in disarray.

He was possessed of anger, and as sometimes happens off the stage, his anger was splendid and glorious to behold. And Tristrem, with the thirst of one who has drunk of thirst itself, caught the cascade of words, and found in them the waters and fountains of life.

"These letters——But how is it possible? God in Heaven——! But can't you see?—the bare idea is an infamy. Your mother was as interested in Raritan as—as——It's enough to make a mad dog blush. It was just a few months before you were born——Bah! the imbecility of Erastus Varick would unnerve a pirate. I know he was always running there, Raritan was, but anyone with the brain of a wooden Indian would have understood——Why, they were here—they came to me, all three of them, and because I knew her father——And precious little thanks I got for my pains. He said he would see the girl in her grave first. He would have it that Raritan was after her for her money. It's true he hadn't a penny—but—what's that got to do with it? The mischief's done. She must have sent these letters to your mother to return to Raritan just before she married that idiot Wainwaring. Your mother was her most intimate friend—they were at school together at Pelham Priory. Raritan, I suppose, was away. Before he got back, your mother—you were born, you know, and she died. She had no chance to return them. That imbecile of a father of yours must have found the letters, and thought—— But how is such a thing possible? Good God! he ought to be dug up and cowhided. And it was for this he left you a Panama hat! And it was for this you have turned over millions to an institution for the shelter of vice! It was for this——See here, since Christ was crucified, a greater stupidity, or one more iniquitous, has never been committed."

In the magnificence of his indignation, Mr. Van Norden stormed on until he lacked the strength to continue. But he stormed to ravished and indulgent ears. And when at last he did stop, Tristrem, who meanwhile had been silent as a mouse, went over to the arm-chair into which, in his exhaustion, he had thrown himself, and touched his shoulder.

"If he did not wish me to have the money," he said, "how could I keep it? How could I?" And before the honesty that was in his face the old man lowered his eyes to the ground. "I am gladder," Tristrem continued, "to know myself his son than to be the possessor of all New York. But when I thought that I was not his son, was that a reason why I should cease to be a gentleman. Though I lost everything else, what did it matter if I kept my self-respect?"

He waited a moment for an answer, and then a very singular thing happened. From Dirck Van Norden's lowered eyes first one tear and then a second rolled down into the furrows of his cheek. From his throat came a sound that did not wholly resemble a sob and yet was not like to laughter, his mouth twitched, and he turned his head aside. "It's the first time since your mother died," he said at last, but what he meant by that absurd remark, who shall say?

For some time Tristrem lingered, lost in thought. It was indeed as he had said. He was gladder to feel again that he was free to love and free to be loved in return than he would have been at holding all New York in fee. As he rose from the nightmare in which he suffocated he did not so much as pay the lost estate the compliment of a regret. It was not that which had debarred him from her, nor was it for that that she had once placed her hand in his. He was well rid of it all, since in the riddance the doors of his prison-house were unlocked. For three months his heart had been not dead but haunted, and now it was instinct with life and fluttered by the beckonings of hope. He had fronted sorrow. Pain had claimed him for its own, and in its intensity it had absorbed his tears. He had sunk to the uttermost depths of grief, and, unbereft of reason, he had explored the horrors of the abyss. And now in the magic of the unforeseen he was transported to dazzling altitudes, to landscapes from which happiness, like the despot that it is, had routed sorrow and banished pain. He was like one who, overtaken by years and disease, suddenly finds his youth restored.

His plans were quickly made. He would go to Narragansett at once, and not leave until the engagement was renewed. He had even the cruelty to determine that his grandfather should come to the Pier himself, and argue with Mrs. Raritan, if argument were necessary.

"I have so much to say," he presently exclaimed, "that I don't know where to begin."

"Begin at the end," his grandfather suggested.

But Tristrem found it more convenient to begin in the middle. He led the old gentleman into the rhyme and reason of the rupture, he carried him forward and backward from old fancies to newer hopes. He explained how imperative it was that with the demolition of the obstacle which his father had erected the engagement should be at once renewed; he blamed himself for having even suggested that Viola was capricious; he mourned over the position in which she had been placed; he pictured Mrs. Raritan's relief when she learned of the error into which she had wandered; and after countless digressions wound up by commanding his grandfather to write an explanation which would serve him as a passport to renewed and uninterruptable favor.

"Certainly—certainly," Mr. Van Norden cried, with the impatience of one battling against a stream. "But even granting that your father wrote to Mrs. Raritan, which I doubt—although, to be sure, he was capable of anything—don't you see that you are in a very different position to-day than you would have been had you not—had you not——"

"You mean about the money?"

"Why, most assuredly I mean about the money," the old gentleman cried, aroused to new indignation by the wantonness of the question.

At this Tristrem, with the blithe confidence of a lover, shook his head. "You don't know Viola," he answered. "Besides, I can work. Other men do—why shouldn't I?"

"And be able to marry when you are ready for the grave. That's nonsense. Unless the young lady is a simpleton, and her mother a fit subject for Bedlam, don't tell them that you are going to work. And what would you work at, pray? No, no—that won't do. You are as fitted to go into business as I am to open a bake-shop."

"I might try stocks," said Tristrem, bravely.

"So you might, if you had the St. Nicholas money to start with. And even then you would have to lose two fortunes before you could learn how to make one. No, if you have not six or seven millions, you will, one of these days—and the later the day the better for me—you will have a few hundred thousand. It is paltry enough in comparison to the property which you threw out of the window, but, paltry or not, it's more than you deserve. Meanwhile, I will——There, don't begin your nonsense again, sir. For the last three months you have done nothing but bother the soul out of me. Meanwhile, if you don't accept what I care to give, and accept it, what's more, with a devilish good grace, I'll—I'll disinherit you myself—begad I will. I'll leave everything I have to the St. Nicholas. It's a game that two can play at. You have set the fashion, and you can abide by it. And now I would be very much indebted if you would let me get some rest."

Therewith the fierce old gentleman looked Tristrem in the eyes, and grasping him by the shoulder, he held him to him for a second's space.

XI.

When Tristrem reached Narragansett he had himself driven to an hotel, where he removed the incidental traces of travel before venturing to present himself at the villa. It was a glorious forenoon, and as he dressed, the tonic that was blown to him through the open window affected his spirits like wine. The breeze promised victory. He had been idle and dilatory, he told himself; but he was older, the present was his, and he felt the strength to make it wholly to his use. The past would be forgotten and put aside; no, but utterly, as Nature forgets—and in the future, what things might be!

"O Magali, ma bien aimée,Fuyons tous deux, tous de—ux——"

The old song came back to him, and as he set out for the villa he hummed it gayly to himself. The villa was but the throw of a stone from the hotel, and in a moment he would be there. He was just a little bit nervous, and he walked rapidly. As he reached the gate his excitement increased. In his breast was a tightening sensation. And then at once he stopped short. On the door of the cottage hung a sign, bearing for legend, "To Let—Furnished."

"But it is impossible," he exclaimed, "they were to be here till October."

He went up and rang the bell. The front windows were closed and barred. The porch on which he stood was chairless. He listened, and heard no sound. He tried the door—it was locked.

"But it is impossible," he kept repeating. "H'm! 'To let—furnished; for particulars apply to J. F. Brown, at the Casino.' Most certainly, I will—most certainly," and monologuing in the fashion that was peculiar to him, he went down the road again, mindful only of his own perplexity.

On reaching the Casino he found that he would have no difficulty in seeing the agent. Mr. Brown, the door-keeper told him, was "right in there," and as he gave this information he pointed to a cramped little office which stood to the left of the entrance.

"Is this Mr. Brown?" Tristrem began. "Mr. Brown, I am sorry to trouble you. Would you be good enough to tell me about Mrs. Raritan's cottage. I——"

"For next summer? Nine hundred, payable in advance."

"I didn't mean about the price. I meant—I was told that Mrs. Raritan had taken it until October——"

"So she did. You can sublet for the balance of the season."

"Thank you—yes—but Mrs. Raritan hasn't gone away, has she?"

"She went weeks ago. There's nothing the matter with the cottage, however. Drainage excellent."

"I have no doubt. But can you tell me where Mrs. Raritan went to?"

"I haven't the remotest idea. Lenox, perhaps. If you want to look at the cottage I'll give you the key."

"I should think——Really, I must apologize for troubling you. Didn't Mrs. Raritan leave her address?"

"If she did, it wasn't with me. When do you want the cottage for?"

Tristrem had not the courage to question more. He turned despondently from Mr. Brown, and passing on through the vestibule, reached the veranda that fronts the sea. In an angle a group of violinists were strumming an inanity of Strauss with perfect independence of one another. Beyond, on the narrow piazza, and on a division of the lawn that leaned to the road, were a number of small tables close-packed with girls in bright costumes and men in loose flannels and coats of diverting hues. At the open windows of the restaurant other groups were seated, dividing their attention between the food before them and the throng without. And through the crowd a number of Alsatians pushed their way, bearing concoctions to the thirstless. The hubbub was enervating, and in the air was a stench of liquor with which the sea-breeze coped in vain.

Tristrem hesitated a second, and would have fled. He was in one of those moods in which the noise and joviality of pleasure-seekers are jarring even to the best-disposed. While he hesitated he saw a figure rising and beckoning from a table on the lawn. And as he stood, uncertain whether or no the signals were intended for him, the figure crossed the intervening space, and he recognized Alphabet Jones.

"Come and have a drink," said that engaging individual. "You're as solemn as a comedian. I give you my word, I believe you are the only sober man in the place."

"Thank you," Tristrem answered; "I believe I do not care for anything. I only came to ask——By the way, have you been here long?"

"Off and on all summer. It's a good place for points. You got my card, didn't you? I wanted to express my sympathy at your bereavement."

"You are very kind; I——"

"But what's this I hear about you? You've bloomed out into a celebrity. Everybody is talking about you—everybody, men, women, and children, particularly the girls. When a fellow gives away a fortune like that! *Mais, tu sais, mon cher, c'est beau, c'est bien beau, ça.*" And to himself he added, "*Et bien bête.*"

Already certain members of immediate groups had become interested in the new arrival, and it seemed to Tristrem that he heard his name circulating above the jangle of the waltz.

"I am going to the hotel," he said. "I wish you would walk back with me. I haven't spoken to a soul in an age. It would be an act of charity to tell me the gossip." Tristrem, as he made this invitation, marvelled at his own duplicity. For the time being, he cared for the society of Alphabet Jones as he cared for the companionship of a bum-bailiff. Yet still he lured him from the Casino and led him up the road, in the hope that perhaps without direct questioning he might gain some knowledge of Her.

As they walked on Jones descanted in the arbitrary didactic manner which is the privilege of men of letters whose letters are not in capitals, and moralized on a variety of topics, not with any covert intention of boring Tristrem, but merely from a habit he had of rehearsing ready-made phrases and noting their effect on a particular listener. This exercise he found beneficial. In airing his views he sometimes stumbled on a good thing which he had not thought of in private. And as he talked Tristrem listened, in the hope that he might say something which would permit him to lead up to the subject that was foremost in his mind. But nothing of such a nature was touched upon, and it was not until the cottage was reached that Tristrem spoke at all.

"The Raritans have gone, I see," he remarked, nodding at the cottage as he did so.

"Yes, I see by the papers that they sailed yesterday."

"You don't mean to say they have gone to Europe. I thought—I heard they were going to Lenox."

"If they were, they changed their plans. Miss Raritan didn't seem up to the mark when she was here. In some way she reminded me of a realized ideal—the charm had departed. She used to be enigmatical in her beauty, but this summer, though the beauty was still there, it was no longer enigmatical, it was like a problem solved. After all, it's the way with our girls. A winter or two in New York would take the color out of the cheeks of a Red Indian. *Apropos de bottes*, weren't you rather smitten in that direction?"

"And you say they have gone abroad?" Tristrem repeated, utterly unimpressed by the ornateness of the novelist's remarks.

"Yes, sir; and were it not that our beastly Government declines to give me the benefit of an international copyright, I should be able to go and do likewise. It's enough to turn an author into an anarchist. Why, you would be surprised——"

Jones rambled on, but Tristrem no longer listened. The position in which he found himself was more irritating than a dream. He was dumbly exasperated. It was his own inaction that was the cause of it all. If he had but bestirred himself sooner! Instead of struggling against that which every throb of his heart convinced him was false, he had dawdled with the impossible and toyed with apostils of grief. At the first obstacle he had turned aside. Where he should have been resolute, he had been weak. He had taken mists for barriers. A child frightened at its own shadow was never more absurd than he. And Viola—it was not surprising that the color had deserted her cheeks. It was no wonder that in his imbecile silence she had gone away. It was only surprising that she had not gone before. And if she had waited, might it not be that she waited expectant of some effort from him, hoping against hope, and when he had made no sign had believed in his defeat, and left him to it. There was no blame for her. And now, if he were free again, that very liberty was due not to his own persistence, but to chance. Surely she was right to go. Yet—yet—but, after all, *it was not too late*. Wherever she had gone he could follow. He would find her, and tell her, and hold her to him.

Already he smiled in scenes forecast. The exasperation had left him. Whether he came to Narragansett or journeyed to Paris, what matter did it make? The errand was identical, and the result would be the same. How foolish of him to be annoyed because he had not found her, in garlands of orange-blossoms, waiting on a balcony to greet his coming. The very fact of her absence added new weight to the import of his message. Yes, he would return to town at once, and the next steamer would bear him to her.

And then, unconsciously, through some obscure channel of memory, he was back where he had once been, in a *Gasthof* in the Bavarian Mountains. It was not yet dusk. Through the window came a choir of birds, and he could see the tender asparagus-green of neighborly trees. He was seated at a great, bare table of oak, and as he raised from it to his lips a stone measure of beer, his eyes rested on an engraving that hung on the wall. It represented a huntsman, galloping like mad, one steadying hand on the bridle and the other stretched forward to grasp a phantom that sped on before. Under the picture, in quaint German text, was the legend, *The Chase after Happiness*. "H'm;" he mused, "I don't see why I should think of that."

"That's the gist of it all," Jones was saying. "It's the fashion to rail against critics. I remember telling one of the guild the other day not to read my books—they might prejudice him in my favor; but in comparison to certain publishers the average reviewer stands as a misdemeanant does to a burglar.

No, I have said it before and I say it again, until that copyright law is passed, the Government is guilty of nothing less than compounding a felony."

Of what had gone before Tristrem had not heard a single word, and these ultimate phrases which reached him were as meaningless as church-steeples. He started as one does from a nap, with that shake of the head which is peculiar to the absent-minded. He was standing, he discovered, at the entrance to the hotel at which he lodged.

"Don't you agree with me?" Jones asked. "Come and lunch at the Casino. You will get nothing here. Narragansett cookery is as iniquitous as the legislature. Besides, at this hour they give you dinner. It is tragic, on my word, it is."

"Thank you," Tristrem answered, elusively. "I have an appointment with— with a train." And with this excuse he entered the hotel, and as soon after as was practicable he returned to town.

It was, he learned, as Jones had said. Mrs. Raritan and Miss Raritan were passengers on a steamer which had sailed two days before. It was then Friday. One of the swiftest Cunarders was to sail the following morning, and it seemed not improbable to Tristrem that he might reach the other side, if not simultaneously with, at least but a few hours after the arrival of the Wednesday boat. Such preparations, therefore, as were necessary he made without delay. As incidental thereto, he went to the house in Thirty-ninth Street. There he learned, from a squat little Irishwoman who came out from the area and eyed him with unmollifiable suspicion, that, like the Narragansett cottage, the house was to let. The only address which he could obtain from her was that of a real-estate agent in the lower part of the city. Thither he posted at once. Yet even there the information which he gleaned was meagre. The house was offered for a year. During that period, the agent understood, Mrs. Raritan proposed to complete her daughter's musical education abroad; where, the agent did not know. The rental accruing from the lease of the house was to be paid over to the East and West Trust Co. Further than that he could say nothing. Thereupon Tristrem trudged hopefully to Wall Street; but the secretary of the East and West was vaguer even than the agent. He knew nothing whatever on the subject of Mrs. Raritan's whereabouts, and from his tone it was apparent that he cared less. There is, however, an emollient in courtesy which has softened greater oafs than he, and that emollient Tristrem possessed. There was in his manner a penetrating and pervasive refinement, and at the gruffness with which he was received there came to his face an expression of such perplexity that the secretary, disarmed in spite of himself, turned from his busy idleness and told Tristrem that if Mrs. Raritan had not left her address with him she must certainly have given it to the lawyer who held the power of attorney to collect the rents and profits of her estate. The name of that lawyer was Meggs, and his office was in the Mills Building.

In the Mills Building Tristrem's success was little better. Mr. Meggs, the managing clerk announced, had left town an hour before and would not return until Monday. However, if there was anything *he* could do, he was entirely at Tristrem's disposal. And then Tristrem explained his errand anew, adding that he sailed on the morrow, and that it was important for him to have Mrs. Raritan's address before he left. The clerk regretted, but he did not know it. Could not Mr. Meggs send it to him?

"He might cable it, might he not?" Tristrem suggested. And as this plan seemed feasible, he gave the clerk a card with a London address scrawled on it, and therewith some coin. "I should be extremely indebted if you would beg Mr. Meggs to send me the address at once," he added; and the clerk, who had read the name on the card and knew it to be that of the claimant and renouncer of a great estate, assured him that Mr. Meggs would take great pleasure in so doing.

After that there was nothing for Tristrem to do but to return to his grandfather's house and complete his preparations. He dined with Mr. Van Norden that evening, and a very pleasant dinner it was. Together they talked of those matters and memories that were most congenial to them; Mr. Van Norden looking steadily in the past, and Tristrem straight into the future. And at last, at midnight, when the carriage came to take Tristrem to the wharf—for the ship was to sail at so early an hour in the morning that it was deemed expedient for the passengers to sleep on board—as Tristrem took leave of his grandfather, "Bring her back soon," the old gentleman said, "bring her back as soon as you can. And, Tristrem, you must take this to her once more, with an old man's love and blessing."

Whereupon he gave Tristrem again the diamond brooch that had belonged to his daughter.

XII.

The journey over was precisely like any other, except in this, that, the tide of travel being in the contrary direction, the number of cabin passengers was limited. Among them there was no one whom Tristrem had met before; yet, after the second day out, there were few whom his appearance and manner had not attracted and coerced into some overture to better acquaintance. Of these his attention was particularly claimed by an Englishman who sat next to him at table, and a young lady who occupied the seat opposite to his own. In the eyes of the latter was the mischievous look of a precocious boy. She was extremely pretty; blonde, fair, with a mouth that said Kiss me—what the French call a *frimousse frottée de champagne*; and her speech was marked by great vivacity. She was accompanied by an elderly person who appeared at table but once, and who during the rest of the voyage remained bundled in shawls in the ladies' cabin, where refreshments were presumably brought her.

It was rumored that this young lady was an ex-star of the Gaiety, and more recently a member of a burlesque troupe that had disbanded in the States. It was added—but then, are not ill-natured things said about everybody? You, sir, and you, madam, who happen to read this page, have never, of course, been spoken of other than with the greatest respect, but what is said of your neighbor? and what have you said yourself?

Tristrem, unaffected by the gossip of the smoking-room, to which, indeed, he lent but an inattentive ear, allowed the young lady to march him up and down the deck and, as was his wont, permitted himself to be generally made use of. Yet if the elderly person in the ladies' cabin had exacted of him similar attentions, the attentions would have been rendered with the same prompt and diligent willingness. He was not a good listener, although he seemed one, but there was a breeziness in the young lady's conversation which helped him not a little to forget the discomforts of ocean travel. He walked with her, in consequence, mile after mile, and when she wearied of that amusement, he got her comfortably seated and, until she needed him again, passed the time in the smoking-room.

It was there that he became acquainted with the Englishman who sat next to him at table. His name, he learned, was Ledyard Yorke. He was an artist by profession, and in the course of a symposium or two Tristrem discovered that he was a very cultivated fellow besides. He seemed to be well on in the thirties, and it was evident that there were few quarters of the globe with which he was not familiar. He was enthusiastic on the subject of French literature, but the manufactures of the pupils of the Beaux Arts he professed to abominate.

"The last time I was at the Salon," he said, one evening, "there were in those interminable halls over three thousand pictures. Of these, there were barely fifty worth looking at. The others were interesting as colored lithographs on a dead wall. There was a Manet or two, a Moreau, and a dozen or more excellent landscapes, but the rest represented the apotheosis of mediocrity. The pictures which Gérôme, Cabanel, Bouguereau, and the acolytes of those pastry-cooks exposed were stupid and sterile as church doors. What is art, after all, if it be not an imitation of nature? To my thinking, the greater the illusion, the nearer does the counterfeit approach the model. And look at the nymphs and dryads which those hair-dressers present. In the first place, nymphs and dryads are as overdone as the assumption of Virgins and the loves of Leda. Besides they were not modern, but even if they were, fancy a girl who lives in the open air in her birthday costume, and who, exposed to the sun, to say nothing of the wind, still preserves the pink and white skin of a baby—and a skin, mind you, that looks as though it had been polished and pinched by a masseur; however, place a dozen of them lolling in conventional attitudes in a glade, or represent them bathing in a pond, and although the sun shines on them through the foliage, be careful not to get so much as the criss-cross of a shadow on their bodies, smear the whole thing with cold cream, label one 'Arcadia,' and the other 'Nymphs surprised,' and you have what they call in France the *faire distingué*."

There was nothing particularly new in what Mr. Yorke had to say, and if, like the majority of men whose thoughts run in a particular channel, he was apt to be dogmatic in his views, he yet possessed that saving quality, which consists in treating the subject in hand not as were it a matter of life and death, but rather as one which is as unimportant as the gout of a distant relative. And it was in the companionship of this gentleman, and that of the young lady alluded to, that Tristrem passed the six days which separated him from the Irish coast.

On the day preceding the debarcation he was in great and expectant spirits, but as the sun sank in the ocean his light-heartedness sank with it. During dinner his charming *vis-à-vis* rallied him as best she might, but he remained unresponsive, answering only when civility made it necessary for him to do so. It is just possible that the young lady may have entertained original ideas of her own on the subject of his taciturnity, but, however that may be, it so happened that before the meal was done Tristrem went up on deck, and seeking the stern of the ship, leaned over the gunwale.

So far in the distance as his eyes could reach was a trail of glistening white. On either side were impenetrable wastes of black. In his ears was the sob of water displaced, the moan of tireless discontent, and therewith the flash and shimmer of phosphorus seemed to invite and tell of realms of enchanted rest beneath. And, as Tristrem watched and listened, the sibilants of the sea gurgled in sympathy with his thoughts, accompanying and accentuating them with murmurs of its own. Its breast was bared to him, it lay at his feet, open-armed as though waiting his coming, and conjuring him to haste. "There is nothing sweeter," it seemed to say, "nothing swifter, and naught more still. I feed my lovers on lotus and Lethe. There is no fairer couch in the world than mine. A sister's kiss is not more chaste. I am better than fame, serener than hope; I am more than love, I am peace. I am unforsakable, and I never forsake."

And as the great ship sped on in fright, it almost seemed to Tristrem that the sea, like an affianced bride, was rising up to claim and take him as her own. Many months later, he thought of the sensation that he then experienced, the query that came to his mind, he knew not how or whence, whether it were not better perhaps—and then the after-shudder as he started back, wondering could it be that for the moment he was mad, and telling himself that in a few hours, a few days at most, he would be with Her. And what had the sea to do with him? Many months after he thought of it.

And as he still gazed at the tempting waters, he felt a hand touch his own, rest on, and nestle in it. He looked around; it was his charming *vis-à-vis* who had sought him out and was now looking in his face. She did not speak; her eyes had lost their mischief, but her mouth framed its message as before. Awkwardly as men do such things, Tristrem disengaged his hand. The girl made one little effort to detain it, and for a moment her lips moved; but she said nothing, and when the hand had gone from her, she turned with a toss of the head and disappeared in the night.

Soon after, Tristrem turned, too, and found his way to the smoking-room. In some way the caress which he had eluded had left a balm. He was as hopeful as before, and he smiled in silent amusement at the ups and downs of his needless fears. In a corner of the room was Yorke.

"I have been looking at the sea," he said, as he took a seat at his side; "it is captious as wine."

"You are a poet, are you not?" Yorke spoke not as though he were paying a compliment, but in the matter-of-fact fashion in which one drummer will say "Dry goods?" to another.

"No; I wish I were. I have never written."

"It's a popular prejudice to suppose that a poet must write. The greatest of all never put pen to paper. What is there left to us of Linus and Musæus? Siddartha did not write, Valmiki did not know how. The parables of the Christ were voiced, not written. Besides, the poet feels—he does not spend a year, like Mallarmé, in polishing a sonnet. De Musset is certainly the best example of the poet that France has to offer; with him you always catch the foot-fall of the Muse—you feel, as he felt, the inspiration. And all the more clearly in that his verses limp. He never would have had time to express himself if he had tried to sand-paper his thoughts. Don't you suppose that Murillo was a poet? Don't you suppose that Guido was? Don't you think that anyone who is in love with beauty must be? I say beauty where I might say the ideal. That is the reason I thought you a poet. You have in your face that constant preoccupation which is distinctive of those who pursue the intangible."

"I am not pursuing the intangible, though," Tristrem answered, with a little sententious nod.

"Ah, who shall say? We all do. I am pursuing it myself, though not in the sense that I attribute to you. Did you ever read Flaubert's *Tentation*? No? Well, fancy the Sphinx crouching at sunset in the encroaching sand. In the background is a riot of color, and overhead a tender blue fading into salmon and the discreetest gray. Then add to that the impression of solitude and the most absolute silence. In the foreground flutters a Chimera, a bird with a dragon's tail and the rainbow wings of a giant butterfly. The Sphinx is staring at you, and yet through and beyond, as though her eyes rested on some inaccessible horizon. Cities crumble, nations rise and subside, and still that undeviating stare! And in her face the unroutable calm of fabulous beauty. I want those eyes, I want that face. You never heard the duo which Flaubert gives, did you? It runs somewhat this way: The motionless Sphinx calls: 'Here, Chimera, rest a while.'

"The Chimera answers: 'Rest? Not I.'

"*The Sphinx.* Whither goest thou in such haste?

"*The Chimera.* I gallop in the corridors of the labyrinth. I soar to the mountain-tops. I skim the waves. I yelp at the foot of precipices. I cling to the skirt of clouds. With my training tail I sweep the shores. The hills have taken their curve from the form of my shoulders. But thou—I find thee perpetually immobile, or else with the end of thy claw drawing alphabets in the sand.

"*The Sphinx.* I am guarding my secret, I calculate and I dream.

"*The Chimera.* I—I am joyous and light of heart. I discover to man resplendent perspectives, Utopias in the skies, and distant felicities. Into his soul I pour the eternal follies, projects of happiness, plans for the future, dreams of fame, and the vows of love and virtuous resolutions. I incite to perilous journeys, to great undertakings. It is I that chiselled the marvels of architecture. It is I that hung bells on the tomb of Porsenna, and surrounded with an orchalc wall the quays of the Atlantides. I seek new perfumes, larger flowers, and pleasures unenjoyed. If anywhere I perceive a man whose mind rests in wisdom, I drop from space and strangle him.

"*The Sphinx.* All those whom the desire of God torments, I have devoured."

Yorke had repeated these snatches from the duo in French. He had repeated them well, bringing out the harmony of the words in a manner which in our harsher tongue would have been impossible. And now he felt parched, and ordered some drink of the steward.

"It is the face of that Sphinx that I want," he continued. "If I were a composer I would put the duo itself to music. I know of no prose more admirable. I have the scene on canvas, all of it, that is, except the Sphinx's face, and that, of course, is the most important. I want a face that she alone could possess. I may find it, I may not. At all events, you see that just at present I too am in pursuit of the intangible. But there, tell me of the artist who is not. It is true, you go to the Academy, and in the Cleopatras and Psyches you recognize the same Mary Jane who the day before offered herself as model to you. My Sphinx, however, was not born in Clapham. Nor does she dwell in Pimlico. But, apropos to Pimlico, I have a fancy that that little friend of yours is on her way to St. John's Wood."

"What little friend?"

"Why, the girl that sits opposite. And what's more to the point, she's in love with you. *Tous mes compliments, c'est un vrai morceau de roi.*"

At this Tristrem blushed in spite of himself. She might have been the Helen for whom the war of the world was fought; she might have been Mylitta or Venus Basilea, and still would she have left him unimpressed. He would not have recognized the divinity—he bowed but to one.

"You remind me," said Yorke, who had watched his expression—"you remind me of De Marsay, who did not know what he did to the women to make them all fall in love with him. There is nothing as fetching as that. And there is nothing, at least to my thinking, that compares with that charm which a woman in love exhales to her lover. It is small matter whether the woman is the daughter of an earl or whether she is a cocotte. There are, I know, people who like their claret in decanters, but so long as the wine is good, what does the bottle matter?

"'*Aimer est le grand point, qu' importe la maitresse?*
Qu' importe le flacon, pourvu qu'on ait l'ivresse?'"

"De Musset was drunk when he wrote that," said Tristrem. "But whether he was drunk or sober, I don't agree with him. I don't agree with him at all. It is the speech of a man who can think himself in love over and over again, and who discovers in the end that through all his affairs he has loved no one but himself."

All of which Mr. Yorke pooh-poohed in the civilest manner, and when Tristrem had finished his little speech, expounded the principles of love as they are formulated in the works of a German metaphysician, supporting them as he did so with such clarity and force of argument that Tristrem, vanquished but unconvinced, left him in disgust.

The next day they were at Liverpool. In the confusion that is incidental to every debarcation Tristrem had had no opportunity of exchanging a word with his *vis-à-vis*. But in the custom-house he caught sight of her, and went forward to bid her good-bye.

"Good-bye," she answered, when he had done so, and putting out her hand, she looked at him with mischievous eyes. "Good-bye," she repeated, lightly, and then, between her teeth, she added, "Imbecile that you are!"

Though what she may have meant by that, Tristrem never understood.

XIII.

It was under cover of a fog of leprous brown striated with ochre and acrid with smoke that Tristrem entered London. In allusion to that most delightful of cities, someone has said somewhere that hell must be just such another place. If the epigrammatist be right, then indeed is it time that the rehabilitation of the lower regions began. London is subtle and cruel, perhaps, and to the meditative traveller it not infrequently appears like an invocation to suicide writ in stone. But whoso has once accustomed himself to its breath may live ever after in flowerful Arcadias and yet dream of its exhalations with regret. In Venice one may coquette with phantoms; Rome has ghosts and memories of her own; in Paris there is a sparkle that is headier than absinthe; Berlin resounds so well to the beat of drums that even the pusillanimous are brave; but London is the great enchantress. It is London alone that holds the secret of inspiring love and hatred as well.

Tristrem sniffed the fog with a sensation of that morbid pleasure which girls in their teens and women in travail experience when they crave and obtain repulsive food. Had he not hungered for it himself? and did she not breathe it too?

The journey from Euston Square to the hotel in Jermyn Street at which he proposed to put up, was to him a confusion of impatience and anticipation. He was sure of finding a cablegram from Mrs. Raritan's attorney, and was it not possible that he might see Viola that very night? In Jermyn Street, however, no message awaited him. Under the diligent supervision of a waiter who had the look and presence of a bishop he managed later to eat some dinner. But the evening was a blank: he passed it twirling his thumbs, dumbly irritated, incapable of action, and perplexed as he had never been before.

The next morning his Odyssey began. He cabled to Mr. Meggs, and saw the clerk put beneath the message the cabalistic letters *A. P.* And then, in an attempt to frighten Time, he had his measure taken in Saville Row and his hair cut in Bond Street. But in vain—the day dragged as though its wheels were clogged. By noon he had exhausted every possible resource. Another, perhaps, might have beguiled the tedium with drink, or cultivated what Balzac has called the gastronomy of the eye, and which consists in idling in the streets. But unfortunately for Tristrem, he was none other than himself. The mere smell of liquor was distasteful to him, and he was too nervous to be actively inactive. Moreover, as in September there are never more than four million people in London, his chance of encountering an acquaintance was slight. Those that he possessed were among the absent ten thousand. They were in the country, among the mountains, at the seaside, on the Continent—anywhere, in fact, except in the neighborhood of Pall Mall. And even had it been otherwise, Tristrem was not in a mood to suffer entertainment. He had not the slightest wish to be amused. Wagner might have come to Covent Garden from the grave to conduct Parsifal in person and Tristrem would not have so much as bought a stall. He wanted Miss Raritan's address, and until he got it a comet that bridged the horizon would have left him incurious as the dead.

On the morrow, with his coffee, there came to him a yellow envelope. The message was brief, though not precisely to the point "*Uninformed of Mrs. Raritan's address*," it ran, and the signature was *Meggs*.

For the first time it occurred to Tristrem that Fate was conspiring against him. It had been idiocy on his part to leave New York before he had obtained the address; and now that he was in London, it would be irrational to write to any of her friends—the Wainwarings, for instance—and hope to get it. He knew the Wainwarings just well enough to attend a reception if they gave one, and a slighter acquaintance than that it were idle to describe.

Other friends the girl had in plenty, but to Tristrem they were little more than shadows. There seemed to be no one to whom he could turn. Indeed he was sorely perplexed. Since the hour in which he learned that his father and Viola's were not the same he had been possessed of but one thought—to see her and kneel at her feet; and in the haste he had not shown the slightest forethought—he had been too feverishly energetic to so much as wait till he got her address; and now in the helter-skelter he had run into a *cul-de-sac* where he could absolutely do nothing except sit and bite his thumb. The enforced inactivity was torturesome as suspense. In his restlessness he determined to retrace his steps; he would return to New York, he told himself, learn of her whereabouts, and start afresh. Already he began to calculate the number of days which that course of action would necessitate, and then suddenly, as he saw himself once more on Fifth Avenue, he bethought him of Alphabet Jones. What man was there that commanded larger sources of social information than he? He would cable to him at once, and on the morrow he would have the address.

The morrow dawned, and succeeding morrows—a week went by, and still no word from Jones. A second week passed, and when a third was drawing to a close and Tristrem, outwearied and enervated, had secured a berth on a returning steamer, at last the answer came—an answer in four words—"Brown Shipley, Founders' Court." That was all, but to Tristrem, in his overwrought condition, they were as barbs of flame. "My own bankers!" he cried; "oh, thrice triple fool! why did I not think of them before?" He was so annoyed at his stupidity that on his way to the city his irritation counterbalanced the satisfaction which the message brought. "Three whole weeks have I waited," he kept telling himself—"three whole weeks! H'm!

Jones might better have written. No, I might better have shown some common-sense. Three whole weeks!"

He was out of the cab before it had fairly stopped, and breathless when he reached the desk of the clerk whose duty it was to receive and forward the letters of those who banked with the house.

"I want Mrs. Raritan's address," he said—"Mrs. R. F. Raritan, please."

The clerk fumbled a moment over some papers. "Care of Munroe, Rue Scribe," he answered.

"Thank God!" Tristrem exclaimed; "and thank you. Send my letters there also."

That evening he started for Paris, and the next morning he was asking in the Rue Scribe the same question which he had asked the previous afternoon in Founders' Court. There he learned that Mrs. Raritan had sent word, the day before, that all letters should be held for her until further notice. She had been stopping with her daughter at the Hôtel du Rhin, but whether or not she was still there the clerk did not know. The Rue Scribe is not far from the Place Vendôme, in which the Hôtel du Rhin is situated, and it took Tristrem a little less than five minutes to get there. The concierge was lounging in her cubby-hole.

"Madame Raritan?" Tristrem began.

"*Partie, m'sieu, partie d'puis hier—*"

And then from Tristrem new questions came thick and fast. The concierge, encouraged by what is known as a white piece, and of which the value is five francs in current coin, became very communicative. Disentangled from layers of voluble digression, the kernel of her information amounted to this: Mrs. Raritan and her daughter had taken the Orient Express the day before. On the subject of their destination she declared herself ignorant. Suppositions she had in plenty, but actual knowledge none, and she took evident pleasure in losing herself in extravagant conjectures. "*Bien le bonjour,*" she said when Tristrem, passably disheartened, turned to leave—"*Bien le bonjour, m'sieu; si j'ose m'exprimer ainsi.*"

The Orient Express, as Tristrem knew, goes through Southern Germany into Austria, thence down to Buda-Pest and on to Constantinople. That Viola and her mother had any intention of going farther than Vienna was a thing which he declined to consider. On the way to Vienna was Stuttgart and Munich. In Munich there was Wagner every other night. In Stuttgart there was a conservatory of music, and at Vienna was not the Opera world-renowned? "They have gone to one of those three cities," he told himself. "Viola must have determined to relinquish the Italian school for the German. H'm," he mused, "I'll soon put a stop to that. As to finding her, all I have to do is go to the police. They keep an eye on strangers to some purpose. Let me see— I can get to Stuttgart by to-morrow noon. If she is not there I will go to Munich. I rather like the idea of a stroll on the Maximilien Strasse. It would be odd if I met her in the street. Well, if she isn't in Munich she is sure to be in Vienna." And as he entered the Grand Hôtel he smiled anew in dreams forecast.

Tristrem carried out his programme to the end. But not in Stuttgart, not in Munich, nor in Vienna either, could he obtain the slightest intelligence of her. In the latter city he was overtaken by a low fever, which detained him for a month, and from which he arose enfeebled but with clearer mind. He wrote to Viola two letters, and two also to her mother. One of each he sent to the Rue Scribe, the others to Founders' Court. When ten days went by, and no answer came, he understood for the first time what the fable of Tantalus might mean, and that of Sisyphus too. He wrote at length to his grandfather, describing his Odyssey, his perplexities, and asking advice. He even wrote to Jones—though much more guardedly, of course—thanking him for his cable, and inquiring in a post-scriptum whether he had heard anything further on the subject of the Raritans' whereabouts. These letters were barely despatched when he was visited by a luminous thought. The idea that Viola intended to relinquish Italian music for that of Wagner had never seemed to him other than an incongruity. "Idiot that I am!" he exclaimed; "she came abroad to study at Milan, and there is where she is. She must have left the Orient Express at Munich and gone straight down through the Tyrol." And in the visitation of this comforting thought Tantalus and Sisyphus went back into the night from which they had come; in their place came again the blue-eyed divinity whose name is Hope.

It is not an easy journey, nor a comfortable one, from Vienna to Milan, but Hope aiding, it can be accomplished without loss of life or reason. And Hope aided Tristrem to his destination, and there disappeared. In all Milan no intelligence of Viola could be obtained. He wrote again to her. The result was the same. "I am as one accursed," he thought, and that night he saw himself in dream stopping passers in the street, asking them with lifted hat had they seen a girl wonderfully fair, with amber eyes. He asked the question in French, in German, in Italian, according to the nationality of those he encountered, and once, to a little old woman, he spoke in a jargon of his own invention. But she laughed, and seemed to understand, and gave him the address of a lupanar.

He idled awhile in Milan, and then went to Florence, and to Rome, and to Naples, crossing over, even, to Palermo; and then retracing his steps, he visited the smaller cities and outlying, unfrequented towns. Something there was which kept telling him that she was near at hand, waiting, like the enchanted princess, for his coming. And he hunted and searched, outwearied at times, and refreshed again by resuscitations of hope, and intussusceptions of her presence. But in the search his nights were white. It was rare for him to get any sleep before the dawn had come.

Early in spring he reached Milan again. He had written from Bergamo to the Rue Scribe, asking that his letters should be forwarded to that place, and among the communications that were given him on his arrival was a cablegram from New York. *Come back*, it ran; *she is here.* It was from his grandfather, Dirck Van Norden, and as Tristrem read it he trembled from head to foot. It was on a Tuesday that this occurred, and he reflected that he would just about be able to get to Havre in time for the Saturday steamer. An hour later he was in the train bound for Desenzano, from which place he proposed to go by boat to Riva, and thence up to Munich, where he could catch the Orient Express on its returning trip to France.

XIV.

When the boat entered the harbor it was already night. Tristrem was tired, but his fatigue was pleasant to him. His Odyssey was done. New York, it is true, was many days away, but he was no longer to wander feverishly from town to town. If he was weary, at least his mind was at rest. Riva is on the Austrian frontier, and while the luggage was being examined Tristrem hummed contentedly to himself. He would get some dinner at the hotel, for he was hungry as he had not been in months. At last he would have a good night's rest; there would be no insomnia now. In the magic of a cablegram that succube had been exorcised forever. On the morrow he would start afresh, and neither stop nor stay till the goal was reached. It was no longer vague and intangible—it was full in sight. And so, while the officers were busy with his traps, he hummed the unforgotten air, *O Magali, ma bien aimée*.

The hotel to which he presently had himself conveyed stands in a large garden that leans to the lake. It is a roomy structure, built quadrangularwise. On one side is a little châlet. Above, to the right and left, precipitous cliffs and trellised mountains loom like battlements of Titan homes. The air is very sweet, and at that season of the year almost overweighted with the scent of flowers. In spite of the night, the sky was visibly blue, and high up in the heavens the moon glittered with the glint of sulphur.

As the carriage drew up at the door there was a clang of bells; an individual in a costume that was brilliant as the uniform of a field-officer hastened to greet the guest; at the threshold was the Oberkellner; a few steps behind him the manager stood bowing persuasively; and as Tristrem entered, the waiters, hastily marshalled, ranged themselves on either side of the hall.

"Vorrei," Tristrem began, and then remembering that he was no longer in Italy, continued in German.

The answer came in the promptest English.

"Yes, my lord; will your lordship dine at *table d'hôte*? Du, Konrad, schnell, die Speise-karte."

Tristrem examined the bill of fare which was then brought him, and while he studied the contents he heard himself called by name. He looked up, and recognized Ledyard Yorke, his companion of months before on the outward-bound Cunarder, who welcomed him with much warmth and cordiality.

"And whatever became of Miss Tippity-fitchet? You don't mean to say you did not see her again? Fancy that! It was through no fault of hers, then. But there, in spite of your promise, you didn't so much as look *me* up. I am just in from a tramp to Mori; suppose we brush up a bit and have dinner together?" He turned to the waiter. "Konrad, wir speisen draussen; verschaffen Sie 'was Monkenkloster."

"Zu Befehl, Herr Baron."

Half an hour later, when the brushing up was done and the Monkenkloster was uncorked, Tristrem and Yorke seated themselves in an arbor that overhung the lake.

"It's ever so much better here than at *table d'hôte*," Yorke began. "I hate that sort of business—don't you? I have been here over two months, but after a week or so of it I gave up promiscuous feeding. Since then, whenever I have been able, I have dined out here. I don't care to have every dish I eat seasoned with the twaddle of cheap-trippers. To be sure, few of them get here. Riva is well out of the beaten track. But one *table d'hôte* is just like another, and they are all of them wearying to the spirit and fatiguing to digestion. Look at that water, will you. It's almost Venice, isn't it? I can tell you, I have done some good work in this place. But what have you been doing yourself?"

"Nothing to speak of," Tristrem answered. "I have been roaming from pillar to post. It's the second time I have been over the Continent, and now I am on my way home. I am tired of it; I shall be glad to be back."

"Yes you were the last person I expected to meet. If I remember rightly, you said on the steamer that you were to be on this side but a short time. It's always the unexpected that occurs, isn't it? By the way, I have got my sphinx."

"What sphinx?"

"I thought I told you. I have been looking for years for a certain face. I wanted one that I could give to a sphinx. The accessories were nothing. I put them on canvas long ago, but the face I never could grasp. Not one of all that I tried suited me. I had almost given it up; but I got it—I got it at last. I'll show it to you to-morrow."

"I am afraid——You see, I leave very early."

"I'll show it to you to-night, then; you must see it. If I had had it made to order it could not suit me better. It came about in such an odd way. All winter I have been at work in Munich. I intended to remain until June, but the spring there is bleaker than your own New England. One morning I said to myself, Why not take a run down to Italy? Two days later, I was on my way. But at Mori, instead of pushing straight on to Verona, I drove over here, thinking it would be pleasanter to take the boat. I arrived here at midnight. The next morning I looked out of the window, and there, right in front of me, in that châlet, was my sphinx. Well, the upshot of it was, I have been here ever since. I repainted the entire picture—the old one wasn't good enough."

"I should like to see it very much," said Tristrem, less from interest than civility.

"I wish you had come in time to see the original. She never suspected that she had posed as a model, and though her window was just opposite mine, I believe she did not so much as pay me the compliment of being aware of my existence. There were days when she sat hour after hour looking out at the lake, almost motionless, in the very attitude that I wanted. It was just as though she were repeating the phrase that Flaubert puts in the Sphinx's mouth, 'I am guarding my secret—I calculate and I dream.' Wasn't it odd, after all, that I should have found her in that hap-hazard way?"

"It was odd," Tristrem answered; "who was she?"

"I don't know. French, I fancy. Her name was Dupont, or Duflot—something utterly *bourgeois*. There was an old lady with her, her mother, I suppose. I remember, at *table d'hôte* one evening, a Russian woman, with an 'itch' in her name, said she did not think she was comme il faut. 'She is comme il *m'en* faut,' I answered, and mentally I added, 'which is a deuced sight more than I can say of you, who are comme il n'en faut pas.' The Russian woman was indignant at her, I presume, because she did not come to the public table. You know that feeling, 'If it's good enough for me, it's good enough for you.' But my sphinx not only did not appear at *table d'hôte*, she did not put her foot outside of the châlet. One bright morning she disappeared from the window, and a few days later I heard that she had been confined. Shortly after she went away. It did not matter, though, I had her face. Let me give you another glass of Monkenkloster."

"She was married, then?"

"Yes, her husband was probably some brute that did not know how to appreciate her. I don't mean, though, that she looked unhappy. She looked impassible, she looked exactly the way I wanted to have her look. If you have finished your coffee, come up to my little atelier. I wish you could see the picture by daylight, but you may be able to get an idea of it from the candles." And as Mr. Yorke led the way, he added, confidentially, "I should really like to have your opinion."

The atelier to which Yorke had alluded as "little" was, so well as Tristrem could discern in the darkness, rather spacious than otherwise. He loitered in the door-way until his companion had lighted and arranged the candles, and then, under his guidance, went forward to admire. The picture, which stood on an easel, was really excellent; so good, in fact, that Tristrem no sooner saw the face of the sphinx than to his ears came the hum of insects, the murmur of distant waters. It was Viola Raritan to the life.

"She guarded her secret, indeed," he muttered, huskily. And when Yorke, surprised at such a criticism, turned to him for an explanation, he had just time to break his fall. Tristrem had fallen like a log.

As he groped back through a roar and turmoil to consciousness again, he thought that he was dead and that this was the tomb. "That Monkenkloster must have been too much for him," he heard Yorke say, in German, and then some answer came to him in sympathetic gutturals. He opened his eyes ever so little, and then let the lids close down. Had he been in a nightmare, he wondered, or was it Viola? "He's coming too," he heard Yorke say. "Yes, I am quite right now," he answered, and he raised himself on his elbow. "I think," he continued, "that I had better get to my room."

"Nonsense. You must lie still awhile."

For the moment Tristrem was too weak to rebel, and he fell back again on the lounge on which he had been placed, and from which he had half arisen. Was it a dream, or was it the real? "There, I am better now," he said at last; "I wonder, I——Would you mind ordering me a glass of brandy?"

"Why, there's a carafon of it here. I thought you had had too much of that wine."

Some drink was then brought him, which he swallowed at a gulp. Under its influence his strength returned.

"I am sorry to have put you to so much trouble," he said collectedly to Yorke and to a waiter who had been summoned to his assistance; "I am quite myself now." He stood up again and the waiter, seeing that he was fully restored, withdrew. When the door closed behind him, Tristrem went boldly back to the picture.

It was as Yorke had described it. In the background was a sunset made of cymbal strokes of vermilion, splattered with gold, and seamed with fantasies of red. In the foreground fluttered a chimera, so artfully done that one almost heard the whir of its wings. And beneath it crouched the Sphinx. From the eyrie of the years the ages had passed unmarked, unnoticed. The sphinx brooded, motionless and dumb.

With patient, scrutinizing attention Tristrem looked in her eyes and at her face. There was no mistake, it was Viola. Was there ever another girl in the world such as she? And this was her secret! Or was there a secret, after all, and might he not have misunderstood?

"Tell me," he said—"I will not praise your picture; in many respects it is above praise—but tell me, is what you said true?"

"Is what true?"

"What you said of the model."

"About her being in the châlet? Of course it is. Why do you ask?"

"No, not that, tell me—Mr. Yorke, I do not mean to be tragic; if I seem so, forgive me and overlook it. But as you love honor, tell me, is it true that she had a child in this place?"

"Yes, so I heard."

"And you say her name was———"

"Madame Dubois—Dupont—I have forgotten; they can tell you at the bureau. But it seems to me———"

"Thank you," Tristrem answered. "Thank you," he repeated. He hesitated a second and then, with an abrupt good-night, he hurried from the atelier and down the corridor till he reached his room.

Through the open window, the sulphur moon poured in. He looked out in the garden. Beyond, half concealed in the shadows, he could see the outline of the châlet. And it was there she had hid! He pressed his hands to his forehead; he could not understand. For the moment he felt that if he could lose his reason it would be a grateful release. If only some light would come! He drew a handkerchief from his pocket and mopped his face. And then suddenly, as he did so, he caught a spark of that for which he groped. The room turned round, and he sank into a chair.

Yes, he remembered, it was at Bergamo, no, at Bologna. Yes, it was at Bergamo, he remembered perfectly well. He had taken from one of his trunks a coat that he had not worn since he went into mourning. It had been warm that day, and he wanted some thinner clothing. He remembered at the time congratulating himself that he had had the forethought to bring it. And later in the day he had taken from the pocket a handkerchief of a smaller size than that which he habitually used. He had looked at it, and in the corner he had found the Weldon crest. As to how it had come in his possession, he had at the time given no thought. Weldon, in one of his visits, might have left it at Waverley Place, or he himself might have borrowed it when dining at Weldon's house. He was absent-minded, he knew, and apt to be forgetful, and so at the time he had given the matter no further thought. After all, what incident could be more trivial? But now the handkerchief, like a magician's rug, carried him back to Narragansett. As well as he could remember, the last occasion on which he wore that coat was the day on which the butler's telegram had summoned him to town. Then, on learning of his father's death, he had put on other things, of sombrer hue. Harris, without rummaging in the pockets, had folded the coat and put it away. And it had remained folded ever since till the other day at Bologna—no, at Bergamo.

That morning at Narragansett, when he was hurrying into the cottage, the man who had aided Viola home the preceding evening drove up with her hat, with this very handkerchief, and the story of a dream. Aye, and his own dream. So this was Truth. She had pursued him, indeed. He could feel her knees on his arms, her fetid breath in his face. But this time it was not a nightmare. It was the real.

Yes, it was that. One by one he recalled the incidents of the past—incidents on which his mind loathed to dwell, rebelling against its own testimony until he coerced the shuddering memories to his will. There were the numberless times in which he had encountered Weldon coming in or leaving her house, almost haunting it with his presence. There was that wanton lie, and the unexplained and interrupted scene between them. It was then, perhaps, that he had first shown the demon that was in him. And then, afterward, was that meeting on the cars—he with a bruise on his cheek and a gash on his neck. Why was Viola's whip broken, if it were not that she had broken it on his face? Why did the nails of her ungloved hand look as though they had been stained with the juice of berries? Why, indeed, if it were not that she had sunk them in his flesh. Why had he heard her calling "Coward" to the night? It was for this, then, that the engagement had been broken; it was for this that she had hidden herself abroad.

For the first time since his boyhood, he threw himself on the bed and sobbed aloud. To stifle his grief he buried his face in the pillow, and bit it with his teeth. It was more than grief, it was anguish, and it refused to be choked. But presently it did leave him. It left him quivering from head to foot, and in its place came another visitor. An obsession, from which he shrank, surged suddenly, and claimed him for its own. In a combat, of which his heart was the one dumb witness, he battled with it. He struggled with it in a conflict that out-lasted hours; but presumably he coped in vain. The next morning his face was set as a captive's. In a fortnight he was in New York.

XV.

The return journey was unmarked by incident or adventure. Nothing less than a smash-up on the railway or the wrecking of the ship would have had the power to distract his thoughts. It may even be that his mind was unoccupied, empty as is a vacant bier, and yet haunted by an overmastering obsession. The ordinary functions of the traveller he performed mechanically, with the air and manner of a subject acting under hypnotic suggestion. One who crossed the ocean with him has since said that the better part of the time the expression of his face was that of utter vacuity. He would remain crouched for hours, in the same position, a finger just separating the lips, and then he would start with the tremor of one awakening from a debauch.

Mrs. Manhattan, who was returning with spoils from the Rue de la Paix, asked him one afternoon, as he happened to descend the cabin-stair in her company, where he had passed the winter.

"Yes, indeed," Tristrem answered, and went his way unconcernedly.

Mrs. Manhattan complained of this conduct to Nicholas, her husband, alleging that the young man was fatuous in his impertinence.

"My dear," returned that wise habitué of the Athenæum, "when a man gives away seven million, it is because he has forgotten how to be conventional."

It was on a Sunday that the ship reached New York, and it was late in the afternoon before the passengers were able to disembark. Tristrem had his luggage passed, and expressed to his grandfather's house, and then, despite the aggressive solicitations of a crew of bandits, started up-town on foot. In the breast-pocket of his coat he carried a purchase which he had made in Naples, a fantastic article which he had bought, not because he wanted it, but because the peddler who pestered him with wares and offers happened to be the best-looking and most unrebuffably good-natured scoundrel that he had ever encountered. And now, at intervals, as he walked along, he put his hand to the pocket to assure himself that it was still in place. Presently he reached Broadway. That thoroughfare, which on earlier Sundays was wont to be one of the sedatest avenues of the city, was starred with globes of azure light, and its quiet was broken by the passing of orange-colored cars. On the corner he stopped and looked at his watch. It was after seven. Then, instead of continuing his way up-town, he turned down in the direction of the Battery. His head was slightly bent, and as he walked he had the appearance of one perplexed. It was a delightful evening. The sky was as blue as the eyes of a girl beloved. The air was warm, and had the street been less noisy, less garish, and a trifle cleaner it might have been an agreeable promenade. But to

Tristrem the noise, the dirt, the glare, the sky itself were part and parcel of the non-existent. He neither saw nor heeded, and, though the air was warm, now and then he shivered.

It seemed to him impossible that he should do this thing. And yet, since that night at Riva, his mind had been as a stage in which it was in uninterrupted rehearsal. If it were unsuccessful, then come what sorrow could. But even though its success were assured, might not the success be worse than failure, and viler to him than the most ignoble defeat? Meditatively he looked at his hand; it was slight as a girl's.

"I cannot," he said, and even as he said it he knew that he would. Had he not said it ten thousand times of times before? It was not what he willed, it was what he must. He was in the lap of a necessity from which, struggle as he might, he could not set himself free. He might make what resolutions he chose, but the force which acted on him and in him snuffed them out like candles. And yet, what had he done to fate that it should impel him to this? Why had he been used as he had? What wrong had he committed? For the past twelvemonth his life had been a continuous torture. Truly, he could have said, "no one save myself, in all the world, has learned the acuity of pain. I alone am its depository."

"And yet," he mused, "perhaps it is right. Long ago, when I was comparing my nothingness to her beauty, did I not know that to win her I must show myself worthy of the prize? She will think that I am when I tell her. Yes, she must think so when it is done. But will it be done? O God, I cannot."

For the instant he felt as though he must turn to the passers and claim their protection from himself. He had stopped again, and was standing under a great pole that supported an electric light. In the globe was a dim, round ball of red, and suddenly it flared up into a flame of the palest lemon, edged with blue. "It is my courage," he said, "I have done with hesitation now." He hailed and boarded a passing car. "Hesitation, indeed!" he repeated. "As if I had not known all through that when the time came there would be none!" He put his hand again to his breast-pocket; it was there.

He had taken the seat nearest to the door, absently, as he would have taken any other, and the conductor found it necessary to touch him on the shoulder before he could extract the fare. He had no American money, he discovered, and would have left the car had not the conductor finally agreed to take his chances with a small piece of foreign gold, though not, however, until he had bit it tentatively with his teeth. It was evident that he viewed Tristrem with suspicion.

At Twentieth Street Tristrem swung himself from the moving vehicle, and turned into Gramercy Park. He declined to think; the rehearsals were over, he did not even try to recall the rôle. He had had a set speech, but it was gone from him as the indecision had gone before. Now he was to act.

He hurried up the stoop of Weldon's house and rang the bell, and as there seemed to him some unnecessary delay, he rang again, not violently, but with the assurance of a creditor who has come to be paid. But when at last the door was opened, he learned that Weldon was not at home.

As he went down the steps again there came to him a great gust and rush of joy. He would go now, he had been fully prepared, he had tried his best. If Weldon had been visible, he would not have hesitated. But he had not been; that one chance had been left them both, and now, with a certitude that had never visited his former indecisions, he felt it was written that that deed should never be done. He gasped as one gasps who has been nearly stifled. The obsession was gone. He was free.

In the street he raised his arms to testify to his liberty reconquered. Yet, even as they fell again, he knew that he was tricking himself. A tremor beset him, and to steady himself he clutched at an area-rail. Whether he stood there one minute or one hour he could not afterward recall. He remembered only that while he loitered Weldon had rounded the corner, and that as he saw him approach, jauntily, in evening dress, a light coat on his arm, his strength returned.

"Royal," he exclaimed, for the man was passing him without recognition. "Royal," he repeated, and Weldon stopped. "I have come to have a word with you."

The voice in which he spoke was so unlike his own, so rasping and defiant, that Weldon, with the dread which every respectable householder has of a scene at his own front door, motioned him up the steps. "Come in," he said, mellifluously, "I am glad to see you."

"I will," Tristrem answered, in a tone as arrogant as before.

"I am sorry," Weldon continued, "Nanny——"

"I did not come to see your wife; you know it."

Weldon had unlatched the door, and the two men passed into the sitting-room. There Weldon, with his hat unremoved, dropped in a chair, and eyed his visitor with affected curiosity.

"I say, Trissy, you're drunk."

"I am come," Tristrem continued, and this time as he spoke his voice seemed to recover something of its former gentleness, "I am come to ask whether, in the purlieus of your heart, there is nothing to tell you how base you are."

Weldon stretched himself languidly, took off his hat, stood up, and lit a cigarette. "Have an Egyptian?" he asked.

"Do you remember," Tristrem went on, "the last time I saw you?"

Weldon tossed the match into an ash-receiver, and, with the cigarette between his teeth, sprawled himself out on a sofa. "Well, what of it?"

"When I saw you, you had just contracted a debt. And now you can liquidate that debt either by throwing yourself in the river or———"

"Charming, Triss, charming! You have made a *bon mot*. I will get that off. Liquidate a debt with water is really good. There's the advantage of foreign travel for you."

"Do you know what became of your victim? Do you know? She went abroad and hid herself. Shall I give you details?"

For the first time Weldon scowled.

"Would you like the details?" Tristrem repeated.

Weldon mastered his scowl. "No," he answered, negligently. "I am not a midwife. Obstetrics do not interest me. On the contra———"

That word he never finished. Something exploded in his brain, he saw one fleeting flash, and he was dead. Even as he spoke, Tristrem had whipped an instrument from his pocket, and before Weldon was aware of his purpose, a knife, thin as a darning-needle and long as a pencil—a knife which it had taken the splendid wickedness of mediæval Rome to devise—had sunk into his heart, and was out again, leaving behind it a pin's puncture through the linen, one infinitesimal bluish-gray spot on the skin, and death.

Tristrem looked at him. The shirt was not even rumpled. If he had so much as quivered, the quiver had been imperceptible, and on the knife there was no trace of blood. It fell from his fingers; he stooped to pick it up, but his hand trembled so that, on recovering it, he could not insert the point into the narrow sheath that belonged to it, and, throwing the bit of embroidered leather in a corner, he put the weapon in his pocket.

"It was easier than I thought," he mused. "I suppose—h'm—I seem to be nervous. It's odd. I feared that afterward I should collapse like an omelette soufflée. And to think that it is done!"

He turned suspiciously, and looked at the body again. No, he could see it was really done. "And so, this is afterward," he continued. "And to think that it was here I first saw her. She came in that door there. I remember I thought of a garden of lilies."

From the dining-room beyond he caught the glimmer of a lamp. He crossed the intervening space, and on the sideboard he found some decanters. He selected one, and pouring a little of its contents into a tumbler he drank it off. Then he poured another portion, and when he had drunk that too, he went out, not through the sitting-room, but through the hall, and, picking up the hat which on entering he had thrown on the table, he left the house.

XVI.

Several thousand years ago a thinker defined virtue as the agreement of the will and the conscience. If the will were coercible the definition would be matchless. Unfortunately it is not. Will declines to be reasoned with; it insists, and in its insistence conscience, horrified or charmed, stands a witness to its acts.

For a fortnight Tristrem had been married to an impulse against which his finer nature rebelled. It was not that the killing of such a one as Weldon was unjustifiable; on the contrary, it was rather praiseworthy than otherwise. His crime was one for which the noose is too good. But to Weldon, in earlier days, he had felt as to a brother; and though affection may die, does it not leave behind it a memory which should thereafter serve as a protecting shield? It had been the bonds of former attachment, bonds long loosened, it is true, but of which the old impress still lingered, that seemed to Tristrem to tie his hands. Then, too, was the horror of such a thing. There is nothing, a Scandinavian poet has said, more beautiful than a beautiful revenge; yet when a man is so tender of heart that if it be raining he will hesitate to shoo a persistent fly out of the window, it is difficult for that man, however great the aggravation, to take another's life. Besides, the impulse which had acted in Tristrem was not one of revenge. He had not the slightest wish to take the law into his own hands. The glaive of atonement was not one which he felt himself called upon to wield. That which possessed him was the idea that until the world was rid of Weldon there was a girl somewhere who could not look her own mother in the face. And that girl was the girl whom he loved, a girl who apparently had no other protector than himself.

In the rehearsals, it was this that had strung his nerves to acting pitch. When it was done he proposed to go to her with a reverence even greater than before, with a sympathy unspoken yet sentiable, and leave her with the knowledge that the injury had been obliterated and the shame effaced. For himself, whatever he may have hoped, he determined to ask for nothing. It was for her he defied the law; he was her agent, one whom she might recompense or not with her lithe white arms, but one to whom she would at least be grateful. And how beautiful her gratitude might be! Though she gave him nothing else, would not the thanks of her eyes be reward enough? And then, as he worked himself up with the thought of these things to acting pitch, then would come the horror of it all, the necessity of taking the life of one who had been his nearest friend, the dread of the remorse which attaches to death, the soiling of his own hands. It was in this fashion that he had wavered between indecision and determination, until, at last, stung by the cynicism of Weldon's speech, there had come to him a force such as he had never possessed before, and suddenly the deed had been done.

The possible arraignment that might follow the inquest, he had never considered. It is said that the art of killing has been lost. The tribunals, assizes, and general sessions have doubtless led somewhat to its discouragement, and yet it must be admitted that the office of police justice in one way resembles that of lover in the tropics—it is not exactly a sinecure. Perhaps, nowadays, it is only the blunderers that are detected; yet, however numerous they may or may not be, Tristrem, without giving a single thought as to how such a thing should be done and remain undetected, had had such chances in his favor that Vidocq himself might have tried in vain to fasten the death of Weldon on him. No one had seen him enter the house, no one had seen him leave it. Even the instrument which he had used, and which he had bought hap-hazard, as one buys a knick-knack, had served his end as cleanly as a paralysis of the heart. It had not spilled a drop of blood.

As Tristrem walked on, he did not think of these things; the possibility of detection had not troubled him, and now the probability that Weldon's death would be attributed to natural causes brought him no satisfaction. Of himself he gave no thought. He had wondered, indeed, that his presence of mind had not deserted him; he had marvelled at his own calm. But now his thoughts were wholly with Viola, and when he reached Fifth Avenue he determined to go to her at once.

A vagabond hansom was loitering near, and with its assistance he presently reached her door. Even as he entered, it was evident that she was not alone. On putting his hat down in the hall he noticed two others, and through the portière came the sound of voices. But he pushed the curtain aside, and entered the room with the air of one to whom the conventional has lost its significance. Yet, as he did so, he felt that he was wrong. If he wished to see Viola, would it not have been more courteous to her to get into evening dress than to appear among her guests in a costume suitable only for the afternoon? Society he knew to be a despot. Though it has no dungeons, at least it can banish, and to those that have been brought up in its court there are no laws rigider than its customs. Besides, was he in a mood to thrust himself among those whose chiefest ambition was to be ornate? He was aware of his mistake at once, but not until it was too late to recede.

Among those present he recognized a man who, though well on in life, devoted his entire time to matters appertaining to the amusements of the selectest circles. He was talking to a girl who, moist as to the lips and eyes, looked as had she just issued from a vapor-bath. Near to her was Mrs. Raritan. Tristrem noticed that her hair had turned almost white. And a little beyond, a young man with a retreating forehead and a Pall Mall accent sat, splendidly attired, talking to Viola.

Mrs. Raritan was the first to greet him, and she did so in the motherly fashion that was her own. And as she spoke Viola came forward, said some simple word, and went back to her former place.

"Come with me," said Mrs. Raritan, and she led him to an S in upholstery, in which they both found seats. "And now tell me about yourself," she added. "And where have you been?"

Truly it was pitiful. She looked ten years older. From a handsome, well-preserved woman she had in a twelvemonth been overtaken by age.

"I have been in Europe, you know," Tristrem answered; "I wrote to you from Vienna, and again from Rome."

"I am sorry," Mrs. Raritan replied; "the bankers are so negligent. There were many letters that must have gone astray. Were you—you had a pleasant winter, of course. And how is your grandfather?"

"I have not seen him. I am just off the ship."

At this announcement Mrs. Weldon looked perplexed.

"Is it possible that you only arrived this evening?" she asked.

"Yes, I wanted to see Viola. You know it is almost a year since—since—I tried to find you both in Europe, but——"

"Mr. Varick, did I hear you say that you arrived from Europe to-day?" It was the gentleman who devoted himself to the interests of society that was speaking.

"Yes, I came on the Bourgogne."

"Was Mrs. Manhattan on board?"

Tristrem answered that she was, and then the gentleman in question entered into an elaborate discourse on the subject of Mrs. Manhattan's summer plans. While he was still speaking a servant informed the vaporous maiden that her maid and carriage had arrived, and presently that young lady left the room. Soon after the society agent disappeared, and a little later the youth that had been conversing with Miss Raritan took his splendor away.

As yet Tristrem had had no opportunity of exchanging a word with Viola. To his hostess he had talked with feverish animation on the subject of nothing at all; but as the adolescent who had been engaging Viola's attention came to Mrs. Raritan to bid that lady good-night, Tristrem left the upholstered S and crossed the room to where the girl was seated.

"Viola," he began, but she stayed his speech with a gesture.

The young man was leaving the room, and it was evident from Mrs. Raritan's attitude that it was her intention to leave it also.

"I am tired," that lady said, as the front door closed; "you won't mind?" And Tristrem, who had arisen when he saw her standing, went forward and bowed over her hand, and then preceded her to the portière, which he drew aside that she might pass.

"Good-night, Mrs. Raritan," he said; "good-night, and pleasant dreams."

Then he turned to the girl. She, too, looked older, or, perhaps, it would be more exact to say she looked more mature. Something of the early fragrance had left her face, but she was as beautiful as before.

Her gold eyes were brilliant as high noon, and her cheeks bore an unwonted color. She was dressed in white, her girdle was red with roses, and her arms and neck were bare.

As Mrs. Raritan passed from the room, Tristrem let the portière fall again, and stood a moment feasting his famished eyes in hers. At last he spoke.

"*He* is dead, Viola."

The words came from him very gravely, and when he had uttered them he looked down at the rug.

"Dead! Who is dead? What do you mean?"

"He is dead," he repeated, but still he kept his eyes lowered.

"He! What he? What are you talking about?" She had left her seat and fronted him.

"Royal Weldon," he made answer, and as he did so he looked up at her.

Her hands fluttered like falling leaves. An increased color mounted to her cheeks, and disappearing, left them white. Her lips trembled.

"I do not understand," she gasped. And then, as her dilated eyes stared into his own, he saw that she understood at last. Her fluttering hands had gone to her throat, as though to tear away some invisible clutch. Her lips had grown gray. She was livid.

"It is better so, is it not?" he asked, and searched her face for some trace of the symptoms of joy. As he gazed at her, she retreated. Her hands had left her throat, her forehead was pinioned in their grasp, and in her eyes the expression of terrified wonder was seamed and obscured by another that resembled hate.

"And it was you," she stammered, "it was you?"

"Yes," he answered, with an air of wonder that equalled her own; "yes——"

"You tell me that Royal Weldon is dead, and that you—that you——"

"It was this way," he began, impelled, in his own surprise, to some form of explanation. "It was this way—you see—well, I went to Riva. That man that brought back your hat——Good God, Viola, are you not glad?"

She had fallen into a chair, and he was at her feet.

"Are you not glad?" he insisted. "Now, it will be——" But whatever he intended to say, the speech remained uncompleted. The girl had drawn from him as from an adder unfanged.

"Assassin!" she hissed. "Assassin!" she hissed again. "What curse——"

"Viola, it was for your sake."

She clinched her hand as though she sought the strength wherewith to strike. And then the fingers loosened again. She moved still farther away. The hatred left her eyes, as the wonder had done before. With the majesty which Mary Stuart must have shown when she bade farewell to England, to the sceptre, and to life, Viola Raritan turned to him again:

"I loved him," she muttered, yet so faintly that she had left the room before Tristrem, who still crouched by the chair which she had vacated, fully caught the import of her words.

"Viola!" he called. But she had gone. "Viola! No, no; it is impossible. It is impossible," he repeated, as he rose up again; "it is impossible."

He staggered to the door and let himself out. And then, as the night-air affects one who has loitered over the wine, he reeled.

In a vision such as is said to visit the ultimate consciousness of they that drown, a riot of long-forgotten incidents surged to his mind. He battled with them in vain; they were trivial, indeed, but in their onslaught he saw that the impossible was truth.

With the aimlessness of a somnambulist, and reasoning with himself the while, he walked down through Madison Avenue until he reached the square. There, turning into Lexington, he entered Gramercy Park. Presently he found himself standing at Weldon's door. "But what am I doing here?" he mused. For a little time, he leaned against the rail, endeavoring to collect his thoughts. Then, as an individual, coated in blue and glistening as to his buttons, sauntered by, he seemed to understand. He left the railing at which he had stood, and, circling the park, set out in the direction of the river. As he reached Second Avenue, a train of the elevated railway flamed about an adjacent corner, and swept like a dragon in mid-air, on, beyond, and out of sight. To the right was a great factory, and as Tristrem continued his way through the unfamiliar street he wondered what the people in the train, what the factory-hands, and the dwellers in the neighborhood would say if they could surmise his errand. The river was yet some distance away. It was such a pity, he told himself, such a pity, that he had not accepted the invitation of the sea. That would have been so much better, so much surer, and so much more discreet. And then he fell to wondering about his grandfather, and his heart was filled with anguish. He would have done anything to save that old man from pain. But it was too late now. A gas-jet that lighted a wide and open door attracted his attention; he looked in, the building seemed empty as a lecture-hall. After all, he decided, perhaps that would be best.

Half an hour later, Tristrem Varick was the occupant of a room that was not as large as one of the closets in his grandfather's house. The furniture consisted of a wooden bench. The sole fixture was an apparatus for drawing water. The floor was tiled and the upper part of the walls was white; the lower, red. The room itself was very clean. There was no window, and the door, which was of grated iron, had been locked from without. From an adjoining cell, a drunken harlot rent the night with the strain of a maudlin ditty.

XVII.

It was some little time before the powers that are could be convinced that Tristrem Varick was guilty of the self-accused murder. It was not that murders are rare, but a murder such as that was tolerably uncommon. The sergeant who presided over the police-station in which Tristrem had delivered himself up was a mild-mannered man, gentle of voice, and sceptical as a rag-picker. He received Tristrem's statement without turning a hair.

"What did you do it for?" he asked, and when Tristrem declined to enter into any explanation, he smiled with affable incredulity. "I can, if you insist," he said, "accommodate you with a night's lodging." And he was as good as his word; but the cell which Tristrem subsequently occupied was not opened for him until the sergeant was convinced that death had really visited the precinct.

Concerning the form in which that death had come, there was at first no doubt. Weldon had been found stretched lifeless on a sofa. The physician who was then summoned made a cursory examination, and declared that death was due to disease of the heart. Had Tristrem held his tongue, that verdict, in all probability, would never have been questioned; indeed, it was not until the minuter autopsy which Tristrem's statement instigated that the real cause was discovered.

It was then that it began to be admitted that violence had been used, but as to whether that violence was accidental or intentional, and if intentional, whether or not it was premeditated, was a matter which, according to our archaic law, twelve men in a pen could alone decide. The case was further complicated by a question of sanity. Granting that some form of manslaughter had been committed, was it the act of one in full possession of his faculties, or was it the act of one bereft of his senses?

Generally speaking, public opinion inclined to the latter solution. Indeed, there seemed to be but one other in any way tenable, and that was, that the blow was self-inflicted. This theory had many partisans. The records, if not choked, are well filled with the trials of individuals who have confessed to crimes of which they were utterly guiltless. It was discovered that a recent slump in Wall Street had seriously affected Weldon's credit. It was known that his manner of living had compelled his wife to return to her father's house, and it was shown that she had begun an action for divorce. It seemed, therefore, possible that he had taken his own life in Tristrem's presence, and that Tristrem, in the horror of the spectacle, had become mentally unhinged.

In addition to this, there was against Tristrem—aside, of course, from the confession—barely a scintilla of evidence. The very instrument which was found on his person, and with which he declared the murder had been committed, was said not to belong to him. A servant of Weldon's thought she had once seen it in the possession of her late master. And it was argued that Tristrem had caught it up when it fell from the hand of the dead, and, in the consternation of the moment, had thrust it in his own pocket. Moreover, as suicides go, there was in Weldon's case a tangible excuse. He was on the edge of bankruptcy, and his matrimonial venture was evidently infelicitous. His life was an apparent failure. Many other men have taken their own lives for causes much minor.

The theory of suicide was therefore not untenable, and those who preferred to believe that a murder had been really committed were at a loss for a motive. Tristrem and Weldon were known to have been on terms of intimacy. Tristrem had been absent from the country a number of months, while Weldon had steadfastly remained in New York. During the intervening period it was impossible to conjecture the slightest cause of disagreement. And yet, no sooner did the two men have the opportunity of meeting, than one fell dead, and the other gave himself up as his murderer. And if that murder had been really committed, then what was the motive?

This was the point that particularly perplexed the District Attorney. It could not have been money. Tristrem had never speculated, and his financial relations with Weldon were confined to certain loans made to the latter, and long since repaid. Nor, through the whole affair, could the sharpest ear detect so much as the rustle of a petticoat. Inasmuch, then, as neither of the two great motor forces, woman and gold, was discernible, it is small wonder that the District Attorney was perplexed. To that gentleman the case was one of peculiar importance. His term of office had nearly expired, and he ardently desired re-election. Two wealthy misdemeanants had recently slipped through his fingers—not through any fault of his own, but they had slipped, none the less—and some rhetoric had been employed to show that there was a law for the poor and a more elastic one for the rich. Now Tristrem's conviction would be the finest plume he could stick in his hat. The possessor of an historic name, a member of what is known as the best society, an habitué of exclusive clubs—a representative, in fact, of everything that is most hateful to the mob—and yet a murderer. No, such a prize as that must not be allowed to escape. The District Attorney felt that, did such a thing occur, he might bid an eternal farewell to greatness and the bench.

But what was the motive of the crime? Long before that question, which eventually assumed the proportions of a pyramid, was seriously examined, it had been demonstrated that the wound from which Weldon had died was not one that could have been self-inflicted. The theory of suicide was thereupon and at once abandoned. And those who had been most vehement in its favor now asserted that Tristrem was insane. What better evidence of insanity could there be than the giving away of seven millions? But apart from that, there were a number of people willing to testify that on shipboard Tristrem's demeanor was that of a lunatic—moreover, did he not insist that he was perfectly sane, and where was the lunatic that ever admitted himself to be demented? Of course he was insane.

A committee, however, composed of a lawyer, a layman, and a physician, visited Tristrem, and announced exactly the contrary. According to their report, he was as sane as the law allows, and, although that honorable committee did not seem to suspect it, it may be that he was even a trifle saner. One of the committee—the layman—started out on his visit with no inconsiderable trepidation. In after-conversation, he said that it had never been his privilege to exchange speech with one gentler and more courteous than that self-accused murderer.

Yet still the motive was elusive. In this particular, Tristrem hindered everybody to the best of his ability. He was resolutely mute.

The attorney who was retained for the defence—not, however, through any wish of Tristrem's—could make nothing of his client. "It is pathetic," he said; "he keeps telling me that he is guilty, that he is sane, that he is infinitely indebted for my kindness and sympathy, *but that he does not wish to be defended.* Sane? He is no more sane than the King of Bavaria. Who ever heard of an inmate of the Tombs that did not want to be defended? Isn't that evidence enough?"

It was possible, of course, to impugn the testimony of the committee, but the attorney in this instance deemed it wiser to let it go for what it was worth, while showing that Tristrem, if sane at the time of the committee's examination, was insane at the time the crime, if crime there were, was committed. It was his settled conviction that if Tristrem would only explain the motive, it would be of such a nature that the chances of acquittal would be in his favor. In this, presumably, he was correct. But, in default of any explanation, he determined that the only adoptable line of defence was the one already formulated; to wit, that in slaying Weldon his client was temporarily deranged.

Meanwhile he expressed his conviction to the grief-stricken old man by whom he had been retained, and who himself had tried, unavailingly, to learn the cause. Whether he divined, or not, what it really was, is a matter of relative unimportance. In any event, he had discovered that on leaving Weldon's house Tristrem, instead of giving himself up at once, which he would have done had he at the time intended to do so at all, had gone directly to Miss Raritan.

And one day he, too, went to her. "You can save him," he said.

He might as well have asked alms of a statue. He went again, but the result was the same. And then a third time he went to her, and on his knees, with clasped and trembling hands, in a voice broken and quavering, he besought her to save his grandson from the gallows. "Come to court," he pleaded; "if you will only come to court!"

"I will come," the girl at last made answer, "I will come to see him sentenced."

Such is the truth about Tristrem Varick. In metropolitan drawing-rooms it was noticed that since Miss Raritan's return from Europe the quality of her voice had deteriorated. Mrs. Manhattan said that for her part she did not approve of the French method.

THE END.

Milton Keynes UK
Ingram Content Group UK Ltd.
UKHW030911151124
451262UK00006B/841